SHE [illegible]
WITHOUT SIN

4/30/20

To Ezra -

May you always have true love, blessed by God.

Martha E Bellinger

MARTHA EMILY BELLINGER

outskirts press

She Who is Without Sin

v2.0

This is a work of fiction. The events and characters described herein are imaginary and are not intended to refer to specific places or living persons. The opinions expressed in this manuscript are solely the opinions of the author and do not represent the opinions or thoughts of the publisher. The author has represented and warranted full ownership and/or legal right to publish all the materials in this book.

Outskirts Press, Inc.
http://www.outskirtspress.com

ISBN: 978-1-9772-0404-2

Library of Congress Control Number: 2018911660

Cover Image by Martha Emily Bellinger
Author Photo by Daily Journal

PRINTED IN THE UNITED STATES OF AMERICA

"'Now in the Law, Moses commanded us to stone such women; what then do You say?' . . . But when they persisted in asking Him, He straightened up, and said to them, 'He who is without sin among you, let him be the first to throw a stone at her'." (John 8: 5, 7, New American Standard Edition, 1977)

DEDICATION

This book is dedicated to all LGBTQpeople who are searching for the true meaning of love, and what is required to maintain such love into eternity.

ACKNOWLEDGMENTS

The author wishes to honor the Creator from whom all creativity flows. The Creator also puts special people in our lives to encourage this creativity. For me, those people include Esther Trickett, my meticulous proofreader and all the women and men in my Claremont California Book Club who have supported my writing endeavors which hopefully are positively opening minds to a new perspective on the LGBTQ community.

CHAPTER ONE

October 13, 1966

"Where the hell is that woman this time," Ruthie muttered to AJ, the Maltese-mix dog she and Ruth had discovered crying outside their bedroom window Easter morning. Dear old Jenny had gone to her heavenly reward shortly after they moved from the farm into their comfortable three-bedroom home in January 1965. It was as if Jenny knew her assignment on earth was done. It had been a blessing for Jenny to die in her sleep, in her warm comfortable bed, at the foot of their bed one snowy day. It was a blessing because Jenny had become so arthritic that Ruthie had taken to carrying her about their home, as well as outside to do "her business."

Ruthie had sobbed when she found Jenny that morning, delaying Ruth's drive to school as together the two women gently wrapped Jenny in what had been her favorite blanket. She was then temporarily put on the work bench in the garage as Ruthie pondered what to do next. Ultimately, although against New York State Cemetery rules, the custodian of the cemetery where Ruthie's parents were buried allowed Jenny's body to be placed in the corner of the mausoleum. When spring arose, Ruthie buried her on the former Stein farm, with Billy's blessing. When Easter rolled around three months later, Ruthie awoke that morning to the whining of a dog outside her window. She got up immediately, looked out the window, and saw a little gray-and-white dog, wagging his tail and crying. Ruth sat up in bed and complained, "It is only 6 a.m., Ruthie, and we don't need to be at church until 9:30. Can't we sleep in for at least another hour?"

"I'm not staying in bed when there's a puppy shivering and whining outside our house," Ruthie scolded.

"What?" Ruth exclaimed, as she rose to look out the window. "Oh my gosh," Ruth shouted. Before anything more could be said, Ruthie was dressed and out the door to retrieve the little guy. She came back into the kitchen with AJ wrapped in an old blanket. "Have you ever seen this dog around Four Corners?" Ruth asked as she prepared some coffee and breakfast, looking in the refrigerator for some food for their Easter-morning visitor.

"No, I have never seen this dog before," Ruthie replied. "He sure is a cute little creature, isn't he? I can't imagine someone just dropping him by the roadside. He must have wandered off from his home. We can ask at church if anyone knows about this little guy's origin. If no one comes forward, maybe we should adopt him." Ruthie held the dog close to her chest and wrapped him even tighter with the blanket.

"Yes. We can ask people at church if he belongs to anyone, and I am all in favor of adoption," Ruth said, as she smiled at Ruthie. Ruth had been suggesting for weeks that Ruthie get a new dog. She thought Ruthie should have a companion through the day while she was away teaching.

Ruthie had some type of special magic with dogs. Ruth watched her teach other people's dogs how to heel, retrieve, sit up, and beg, as well as shake hands and roll over. Of course, Jenny had been the best proof of how a human being and a dog could be in perfect harmony with one another. Between Jenny's natural intelligence and Ruthie's incredible patience, Jenny had learned a phenomenal number of commands. *Maybe this little fellow will do the trick and capture Ruthie's heart*, Ruth thought. After all, it was Easter morning and surely, it was a sign that Ruthie's love for a new dog had been resurrected.

Tonight, however, as Ruthie swore to herself about Ruth's tardiness, AJ had looked her straight in the eye and then run to the back door, awaiting Ruth's arrival. It was 6:30 p.m., and no Ruth. School got out each day at 3:00 p.m., but Ruthie accepted the fact that Ruth's vice-principal responsibilities sometimes made it impossible for her to get home before 5:30. That was the time they had agreed they would have dinner together each night, and Ruthie agreed she would cook for them. However, for the past six weeks, Ruth had been late at least once a week getting home for dinner. It was now 6:45, and the special meal Ruthie had prepared from a new recipe—chicken and rice casserole, with a side of string beans—had been simmering on the stove for well over an hour. The string beans had long since died.

Ruthie thought about the fact that Ruth had promised, long ago, she would call Ruthie right after 3 p.m. if she was going to be very late, but she never did. For the past few weeks, Ruth was late for dinner at least once a week. There was no pattern to Ruth's tardiness for dinner. The tardiness had occurred on different days of the week. Ruthie began to contemplate that Ruth was involved in something she did not want Ruthie to know about. She had no reason to distrust Ruth's fidelity, and Ruthie had to admit to herself that she was as jealous of Ruth's time as much as Ruth's affection.

She thought about what a "grand dame" Ruth had become in Four Corners. Since her significant raise from the vice principal's job, Ruth had purchased some exquisite executive suiting, as well as silk blouses. Ruth went out the door of their home every day looking like a million dollars. Most days, Ruthie would just smile and stare at Ruth as she started out the door, with Ruth always inquiring of Ruthie if something was amiss in her dress. "What are you staring at, Ruthie? Do I have a run in my stocking, or is my slip sticking out below my skirt?" Ruth had inquired more than once.

On one occasion, Ruthie had declared, "No, my dear, you look fabulous as ever. Don't you think it's a good thing that I still occasionally stare at you, with love and lust after fourteen years together?" Ruth had responded, on that occasion, by walking back to the kitchen table and giving Ruthie a quick kiss as she dashed out the door.

The first year in their new home, Ruthie had kept herself busy fixing things around the house and doing some renovation, as well as painting and wallpapering two of the bedrooms. She went to the grocery store twice a week to get the items she needed for their meals. Every night when Ruth got home, she would proudly show Ruth the latest project she had completed. Ruth would always express her gratitude. Once Ruth joked, "Well, there you go again, saving us all this money we would be spending for repairmen. You are a wonder; you can do anything a man can do, except with you, I don't have to pretend to have a headache on Friday or Saturday night!" resulting in a good laugh from both women.

Yes, Ruthie could fix anything, except the broken heart she had for the loss of her beloved farm and animals. Deep down, Ruth knew Ruthie was unhappy and restless. She had attempted to get her to go back to school at the community college in Watertown, but Ruthie would not hear of it.

"I am forty-six now, and I'd be twice the age of any student there. Besides, think of all the gas money we would spend with me driving back and forth to Watertown at least three days a week. Who would fix our dinner every night? And what would poor AJ do? He'd be alone all day," Ruthie would argue.

Ruth had given up arguing the subject of continuing education. She knew Ruthie was trying to be a good sport about their role reversal. She knew about the morning Ruthie had arranged for Cindy to come over for coffee and help Ruthie learn more about cooking.

"How great it is that you are so eager to learn how to cook and relieve Ruth of that duty," Cindy observed. "I've often thought to myself how wonderful it would be to come into the house with a home- cooked meal awaiting me. Seems to me, all of us women could use a wife now and then," Cindy said, as she took a big sip of Ruthie's coffee. "Well, coffee-making will not be something I need to teach you. Billy and Ruth always said you make the best coffee, and they were right."

Cindy had arrived that morning with a copy of *The Joy of Cooking,* which she told Ruthie was the best cookbook ever written. You could look up and find a recipe for any dish, bread, or dessert you wanted to make, she had reassured Ruthie. "It is okay to experiment, too," Cindy said. "So what, if the casserole or dessert doesn't come out quite right? When you taste it, you will figure out what you did wrong. You might find out that your experimentation with ingredients and combinations made the dish taste even better.

"I learned a few things about basic cooking from my mother and through the home economics classes as well. I like cooking and wanted to expand my menu for Billy, and now the kids."

Ruthie smiled as she remembered that within a year of their marriage in 1953, Cindy had given birth to a boy, William Packer, Jr. Then in 1955, Ellen Ruth Packer had arrived March 2, the day after Ruthie's 35th birthday, and the proud parents gave her the middle name of "Ruth." Billy's mother had been annoyed with that middle name for her granddaughter. She had thought they would give Ellen her paternal grandmother's first name, "Elizabeth." Ruth and Ruthie were so happy with little Ellen, and not a birthday went by that there wasn't a joint celebration of Ruthie's and Ellen's birthdays, even if it was a second celebration for Ellen. Ellen really liked her "aunts" and took a liking to Ruthie, who was always ready to put Ellen on her knee and read her a story or take a long walk with her and the dog. During these walks, Ruthie often pointed out many things about the animals and plants they saw along the way, and when she got back home, Ellen would excitedly tell her parents about a unique stone she had found or pretty leaf in the autumn months. William, "Billy Junior," as they called him, was in love with Ruth because of her fabulous baking abilities and was content to sit in the kitchen with a glass of milk and a couple of warm cookies while his sister went out wandering with Ruthie. Ruth and Ruthie often served as babysitters for the two children, who were always asking their parents, "Can we go over to our aunts' house, please?" when they became bored with the events at their own home.

After pondering these thoughts about the kids, Ruthie spoke up. "Well, the title of this cookbook is a hoot to me because I find little joy in cooking, and I doubt Ruth or anyone else has ever found much joy in what I cook! To me, it is a necessary evil; always has been, always will be. I think my mother understood that, now that I look back over my time on the farm. My mother would scowl when I would come home from high school and my only grade, other than A, was in home economics, with a passing C. It was the only C grade I had ever gotten. If only the school had let me take woodshop along with the boys, it would have been an A. Father laughed when he saw that home economics grade and said, 'Your future husband may have to do the cooking while you milk the cows, Ruthie.'"

Ruthie remembered replying to her father, "There will be no need for cooking, Father, because I am not going to get married."

To that announcement her father had said, "Well, you will get married if Billy Packer has anything to do about it. He always smiles broadly when he sees you, and I can just see the two of you working, side by side, in the barn and fields until some children come along."

Ruthie smiled at Cindy, sharing the memory. "Thankfully for all concerned, that marriage never came to pass. He never could have gotten a better wife than Cindy Adams."

"And you could never have found a better companion than our cousin Ruth. Things have been a little rough for you two these last two years, but you both seem flexible enough to make your relationship work," Cindy said.

"I guess we are doing okay, although it has been hard for me to readjust to basic household duties. I've tried to fill some of my time with maintenance and renovation projects. When I cook something for Ruth, I try to remember it is another expression of my love and support. However, I do confess my mind is usually preoccupied with thinking about what I can do as 'Miss Fixit,' and the evening meal gets overdone sometimes."

Cindy laughed loudly and took Ruthie's hand. "We never talk about it, Ruthie, but I know, in your own way, that you and Ruth are as much married as Billy and me. I think you know Billy and I are so happy you found each other. So, as one wife to another, cooking, cleaning, doing laundry is often the last thing most of us want to do. You know me. I'd rather hop in the car and go to Watertown shopping for clothes, sitting at the counter of Woolworth's having a hot dog and crème soda, and maybe stopping by the Arcade for some caramel corn. Just getting out where there are more people, and sometimes not seeing anyone you know, is so refreshing to me. When I get downcast from these household duties, I tell myself I will be going for a day trip to Watertown soon, and as the good Lord said, 'This too shall pass.'

"Now, let's plan a special dinner tonight for Ruth by seeing what you have in the refrigerator and the freezer. It should be a dish you've never made before, and we will use *The Joy of Cooking* for a recipe."

As Ruthie remembered this talk with Cindy, she looked at the clock. It was now 6:45, and no Ruth. Ruthie didn't know if she was more worried about Ruth's safety or angry at her tardiness. Just at that moment, she heard Ruth's car in the driveway.

Ruthie went to the stove and stirred the food again to keep it from burning. Ruth bounded in the door, smiling, but Ruthie certainly did not think the occasion warranted a smile. "Now, just where have you been?" Ruthie scolded in such a loud voice that AJ hid under the kitchen table and peered out from under the tablecloth at Ruth. He had heard that tone in Ruthie's voice only once before, and he didn't like it. "Dinner has been simmering on this stove for well over an hour, and there was no call to me about your being so late," Ruthie snapped.Ruth had anticipated this might well be the response she would get when she walked in the door. However, it was the accusing inflection in Ruthie's voice that Ruth had never heard before. The tone went beyond annoyance and sounded like a Nuremburg trial interrogation. She wasn't quite sure how to reply. She could not tell Ruthie why she was so late, and she knew it was unfair to Ruthie's cooking efforts to have been so tardy without an earlier call telling Ruthie that she would be late.

Ruth pleaded her case. "My goodness, Ruthie. Don't be so mad. I am sorry for being late, but I've told you before, things at school sometimes hold me up."

"Yes, you've said that a lot lately, and being late for dinner is occurring at least once a week. What's changed from previous school- year hours that I don't know about?" Ruthie demanded.

"Now you are making me very angry, Ruthie. Do you remember all the meals I had to delay when we were on the farm because of some emergency in the barn? Did I ever confront you or fail to accept your explanation for why we needed to delay dinner? I knew you would understand. Surely you can see that the vice principal's job often includes hours of work after the school has let out," Ruth said.

"This is a different situation from barn emergencies, and you know it," Ruthie spat back in a somewhat lowered tone of voice so that AJ would come out from under the table. "We can discuss this more later, but you might as well sit down and eat what is left of the dinner that has been simmering on the stove for an hour and a half. I am not even going to serve you the string beans. They are ruined."

The two women proceeded to eat their meal in icy silence. Neither felt like trying to make things better between them. As usual, Ruth got up after the meal was finished and started clean-up. In a sarcastic tone, Ruthie told her it was unnecessary for her to do the dishes. "I know this is my role, now," Ruthie said. She told Ruth to adjourn to the living room and read the *Watertown Daily Times.*

Ruth complied and set her dishes down in the sink, walking off to the living room. AJ trailed into the living room with his second mom and jumped up on the couch next to her as she read through the *Times.* Ruth knew it was better to drop this discussion about her tardiness with Ruthie. She'd never be late again unless she called ahead of time.

Ruth lay in bed that night going over every detail of the eventful day. In her mind, she and Ruthie were now living the opening phrases of *The Tale of Two Cities.* It was literally the best of times and the worst of times for the two of them. It was the worst of times because switching roles had been incredibly difficult for Ruthie. Ruthie was clearly unhappy being home alone. She also had learned over the fourteen years of their relationship that Ruthie craved Ruth's undivided attention. If anything interrupted their time together, it had to be eliminated. Work, of course, was an exception, with Ruthie frequently telling Ruth how proud she was of her accomplishments, especially by becoming a vice principal, which just didn't happen—in these parts, at least. Ruthie often said she knew Ruth needed the intellectual stimulation of teaching and talking to her colleagues on the faculty about the affairs of the day. There was, however, nothing else Ruthie would allow to intrude upon their life together.

How would they get through this rough road they were now traveling? She felt uncomfortable discussing her tardiness this evening, because she knew Ruthie would make much more out of it than it was. Ruth needed more people in her life than just the faculty, students, and church members. Ruthie was a loner, really. Billy had warned Ruth that Ruthie was a very good woman, but not a friend- maker like his cousin. "I'll be interested in seeing if you can get her to go anywhere or associate with anyone who doesn't live in Four Corners," Billy had chuckled. "Then again," Billy said, "if anyone can change her, it would be you; she adores you so."

How right Billy had been. Ruthie discouraged any social life with other women outside church circles. Even their one lesbian friend, June, the physical education teacher, was a threat to Ruthie even though Ruth had told Ruthie a thousand times that she was not attracted to June "in that way." So, the couple stopped having June over for dinner once a month, and Ruth continued to have lunch with June at school.

Conversely, it was the best of times for them financially. Ruth was now tenured, and they did not have to rely on a sometimes unpredictable farm income. Ruthie did her part, as well, by fixing everything that needed to be fixed around the house, installing new gadgets like their garbage disposal. This saved them so much money on repairmen, and thanks to Ruthie purchasing their home outright, they had no mortgage. This allowed them to have two cars and put some money into savings. Ruth had to admit she liked having the money for the new outfits she wore at school and church, as well as buying costume jewelry from time to time. She didn't have to think twice about buying perfume or cosmetic supplies.

Ruth knew, however, that this updated version of herself worried Ruthie a lot. Ruth knew from Ruthie's joking comments that she was afraid Ruth would tire of their relationship and seek "some cuter, younger, more erudite" woman to replace Ruthie. Ruth always cut off Ruthie's jokes about this happening by saying, "Oh, don't be ridiculous."

A couple times a year, Ruthie would allow Ruth to drag her into Watertown for some new clothes. Ruthie would purchase the now popular women's slacks, with blouses that matched, as well as sweaters and in the winter, turtlenecks. Ruth also insisted Ruthie get new blazers from time to time. Ruthie was quite capable of making a good appearance herself, and when she did, Ruth always smiled and complimented Ruthie. Together, the two women always appeared well dressed and happy when out in the community, but things were not altogether happy at home. Ruthie sensed Ruth had given up on their sexual relationship many years ago when she had begun to tell Ruth that she was "too tired from all the farm chores, and couldn't we just cuddle." Now that they were off the farm, Ruthie had tried to renew this intimacy, but now it was Ruth saying, "It's been such a hectic week at school, how about a cuddle?" With that question, Ruth would say, "You know I love you, don't you?" She would then place her head on Ruthie's shoulder and drift off to sleep.

Ruthie told herself that deep down inside, she knew Ruth loved her, and she should be content with the fact that "her girl" still enjoyed falling asleep on her shoulder. Yet, the memory remained of their early days together, when they just couldn't get enough of each other despite exhausting farm work, and later, teaching duties for Ruth. Maybe this was what happened to all couples after fourteen years together, whether they were heterosexual or homosexual. There was no one to talk to about this stuff for a lesbian couple, so she just accepted that it was the way it had to be.

CHAPTER TWO

John Packer was a hard worker on the now expanded farm operation after the acquisition of the Stein farm. However, unlike his brother Billy, he had not married well. His wife, Alice, was a very unhappy woman who was a witch at home, but a smiling, attractive woman in public settings. It was essential to Alice that John secured for her materially everything that Billy and Cindy had acquired in their marriage, and she never let up about John demanding his fair share of the Packer farm earnings. John trusted Billy implicitly. He had no reason to distrust Billy, because Billy worked so hard to lessen John's load. His older brother could see how unhappy John was in his marriage and encouraged his brother to stand up for himself with Alice. Whenever an errand needed to be run, Billy always sent John, so he could get away from Alice for even a few hours.

Today, the errand was near Clayton, and Billy had suggested John take his time and, maybe, have a hamburger and some fries at a diner. There were at least three choices for hamburger joints, but John wanted to give fish 'n' chips a try. As he pulled his truck in front of the diner, he was surprised, but happy, to see Ruth's red Falcon parked in front as well. Had she dashed home to get Ruthie for a meal out? That would be like Ruth. His sister-in-law, Cindy, had expressed that Ruthie was having a very difficult time switching from farmer to homemaker. No doubt Ruth would try as often as she could to treat Ruthie to a meal out. John was proud of his cousin as a brilliant woman and good human being.

As he was just about to open the diner door, he heard a very loud jukebox playing "Blue Suede Shoes," with people clapping loudly and cheering. What on earth was happening here? He stepped into the bar area of the diner that overlooked a small dance floor. No one paid any attention to his entrance because they were transfixed on a man and woman dancing. He looked closer and realized that his beloved cousin, Ruth, and Principal Slater were jitterbugging up a storm! He quietly sat on a bar stool in utter amazement. They were fabulous dancers! But what was his cousin doing here at 4 p.m. without Ruthie? He had always known, through Billy, that Ruth and Ruthie were more than housemates, but at Billy's urging, he had never said a word to anyone. Did Ruthie know about this? The music on the jukebox switched to "In the Mood," and Principal Slater grabbed Ruth's hand and they moved elegantly into swing dancing as if they had been dancing partners forever.

John knew he needed to unobtrusively exit the diner without Ruth seeing him. He'd have his hamburger somewhere else and think over this situation and what, if anything, he should mention to anyone. He knew he would not tell his wife, because she had become the most vicious gossip in all of Four Corners. Alice would be the first one to try and sully Ruth's reputation, for she was immensely jealous of Ruth's brilliance, skill on the piano, and marvelous wardrobe choices. Everyone at church loved Ruth, and Ruth seemed at home with just about anyone. "Just who does she think she is?" Alice had once said. "She comes into this community, a stranger, and flaunts herself about as if she'd lived here all her life," Alice complained. John had responded that he did not see his cousin as flaunting anything. In fact, Ruth was very humble about mentioning anything concerning herself. Alice had responded, "You would say that because she's your cousin, and you Packers all stick together."

John got back in his truck and drove to the Halfway House diner, where he ordered the cheeseburger special and coffee. As he sat at the counter, the scene he witnessed fifteen minutes before made no sense to him whatsoever. Ruth was a very good-looking woman, and he did agree with his wife that his cousin was the best-dressed woman around. She always matched some clip-on earrings to the color of her outfit. In contrast to Ruthie, who liked to dress in blue jeans, dress slacks, and comfortable shoes, Ruth often matched her shoes with the color of her always feminine outfit.

Many in the community still wondered why she didn't get married and continued to live with Ruthie. Maybe Billy was wrong about their cousin, and Ruth wanted more out of life? Maybe she wanted the social life a man could provide. He had high regard for Ruthie, but he had to admit Ruthie was a "stick in the mud." Oh my God! He wanted to talk to Ruth in person and get her version of these events, but when could he get away from his wife long enough to talk to her? He usually could talk to his brother about anything—but this?

Once a month, Billy and Cindy went to Ruth and Ruthie's home for dinner and to play pinochle. By Billy's account, it was always a wonderful evening filled with good food, many laughs, and easy- listening music in the background playing on a new phonograph they now called a stereo. Billy said it was a night off from cooking for Cindy, and she never got tired of Ruth's witty comments about life in Four Corners. That was the solution—he'd talk to his sister-in-law! She had frequently dropped by their home during the work week for coffee with Ruthie, and she often went shopping with Ruth in Watertown. She would know what to think about this situation and how to tell Ruth she had been seen by John, dancing up a storm with Principal Slater. Ruth had to be told because if he had run into her, she was risking being seen by other Four Corners residents.

When he arrived back at the farm, Billy and the hired hand they had recently employed for milking and feeding, were just finishing the evening chores. "Hi, brother," Billy yelled. "Did you enjoy your afternoon free of Alice?"

"Sure did, Billy, thanks," John replied in a muted voice.

"You look so serious," Billy replied. The two brothers were more like twins, and they could read each other like a book. Right then, John realized he had to tell Billy first about what he had seen. Billy still had Ruthie on a pedestal from their forty-plus years of being friends, and he probably knew Ruthie better than anyone, except Ruth. Billy was so proud of his cousin Ruth's accomplishments; he'd understand that protecting her reputation was paramount, as well as sparing Ruthie from hearing any gossip.

There were a few prudish people in their church who might find it good that Ruth was dating Paul but would be aghast to know, of all things, that they went dancing right after school on week nights to the sounds of a jukebox located in an establishment which sold liquor. There was a time that good Methodists looked down upon dancing, and drinking alcohol was really frowned upon. He didn't feel that way, but he didn't want his cousin to be hurt by unkind things which might be talked about behind her back.

"If you have a minute for me, I'd like to talk to you about something, Billy," John asked.

"Let me see if I can guess what it is you want to discuss," John rubbed his chin as if he was in deep thought. "You had an afternoon away from Alice, and it's got you thinking about divorce. No, no—that can't be it, because we Packers never divorce. Believe me, brother, my heart aches for you, and I'd be standing right beside you if you did leave her. Perhaps she's convinced you that you need more of the Packer farm proceeds? Maybe the stork is about to drop another bundle at your house?"

"Actually, I'd take any one of those choices if I had to, but what I need to talk about is very confusing and difficult to discuss."

Billy suggested they sit down on some bales of hay and became very serious himself. "So, just be out with it, John. No use hemming and hawing about this with me. You know you can tell me anything in confidence."

"Okay then," John began. "I followed your suggestion about going into Clayton for a late lunch. I decided to try that Dave's Fish 'n' Chips place right on the river. I pulled up behind Ruth's Falcon and looked at my watch. It was 4 p.m. and I just couldn't figure out what she'd be doing in Clayton. At first, I thought she might have dashed home, picked up Ruthie, and they were having a nice little dinner overlooking the Islands. As I was entering the joint, I heard the jukebox playing 'Blue Suede Shoes,' and people were clapping and shouting as two dancers were twirling about doing the best jitterbugging I've ever witnessed.

"I sat down on a bar stool to watch and immediately saw the two dancing were Ruth and Principal Slater. Both had taken off their jackets and were just cutting up the rug. The music on the jukebox changed to 'In the Mood,' and Paul just swept Ruth into his arms and they were off again, this time swing dancing. It was as if they had been dancing partners forever, they were so good. Apparently, the dozen other patrons, as well as the bartender, thought so, too, because they were all egging them on to keep dancing. I didn't want Ruth to see me, so I slipped out the door before the second song ended. Could they possibly be in a dating relationship?" John asked.

Billy didn't answer immediately; he just stared at John. Finally, he responded. "I sure hope that isn't the case, for Ruthie's sake. I want to believe our cousin has more integrity than that. There are people who walk on both sides of the street, you know. That happens much more with homosexual men, but I suppose it goes for women, too. Ruth is a good-looking woman. We've talked about that before. Paul Slater is very handsome and a Harvard man, out with a woman who graduated at the top of her class from Smith. It makes sense they would be attracted to one another. Yet, Cindy and I were just over to the girls' home last Saturday night, and they seemed perfectly at ease with one another. Nothing was amiss; in fact, Ruth seemed particularly affectionate with Ruthie, grabbing Ruthie's hand during dinner and when we were playing cards. Ruth even gave Ruthie a big hug when she got up to clear the dinner dishes and told the three of us to go on in the living room to set up the card table. It is hard to conceive of Ruth being so devious, especially in the love department," Billy concluded.

"If Ruth was unusually affectionate to Ruthie last Saturday night, maybe she was feeling guilty," John suggested.

"Again, I just don't see our cousin being insincere like that. It is very curious though, John, I'll give you that. I need to think about this overnight. We should not spread any gossip about this, and I don't need to tell you, John, that if Alice hears about this, Ruth and Ruthie will both be hurt. There could be an absolutely innocent explanation for what you saw, and I'm going to keep believing that until I hear otherwise from Ruth or Ruthie," Billy said.

"I agree, Billy. It is none of our business as to what is going on. Don't worry; Alice is the last person I would ever tell this story to," John said. With that, both brothers headed off to their respective farmhouses.

Billy was brooding all during supper that night. Cindy rarely saw her husband in less than a pleasant disposition. She asked him if he felt sick, and he said he felt very sick, in a sarcastic tone. After their thirteen years together, she knew they needed to have an adult conversation without the kids around. She concentrated on getting the kids fed and reminded them they had homework to do. She bribed them with promises of a bowl of ice cream once they had showed her their homework. With that, they bounded upstairs to their bedrooms.

"Okay, honey, out with it. What's making you so glum?"

"Truthfully, Cindy, I'm not sure if I'm dazed, amazed, or crazed," Billy said. "I sent John today on an errand to the Reece farm to pick up the new Surge milking machines we're buying from them. Since it was so near Clayton, I told him to take his time and maybe grab a burger, anything to get John away from Alice for a few hours, you know. He ended up at Fish 'n' Chips, parking right behind Ruth's red Ford Falcon, finding it strange she was there at 4 p.m. on a Wednesday."

Billy proceeded to tell Cindy every detail of John's brief time at Fish 'n' Chips. He then hung his head and asked Cindy for some more coffee. Cindy, without saying a word, got the coffee pot and poured Billy coffee with her right hand, as she gently rubbed his shoulder with her left. She needed a moment to process all this extraordinary information.

Finally, in a hushed voice, she spoke. "Well, what a story! I understand why you could be worried and upset. Yet, it just seems so unlike your cousin to be dancing like she was on *American Bandstand* right after school hours, with Principal Slater. I suppose she is capable of being a 'free spirit,' as they say now. I also know from talking privately with both Ruth and Ruthie that they adore one another, at least that's what I thought. Finally, if there was ever a woman who was without sin, it must be Ruth. I can't remember one dishonest thing she has done in the years I have known her." Cindy slid back into her chair, after filling her own coffee cup, and just stared at her husband as she thought some more about this situation.

She continued, "I mean, we both saw how affectionate Ruth was toward Ruthie last Saturday night. We even talked about that on the way home, remember? We both agreed they were a fine example of hanging in there together, even when things had totally upset the apple cart for them. I just refuse to believe your cousin would do anything behind Ruthie's back. How do we know this wasn't a totally innocent spur of the moment event intended to burn off some stress from the school day? Is it even fair for us to assume Ruthie knows nothing about this?"

"I expressed the same thoughts to John, but he pointed out that maybe Ruth was unusually solicitous to Ruthie this past Saturday because Ruth was feeling guilty. We can agree that Ruth Packer and Paul Slater make an attractive couple. Ruth may be a bit older than Paul, but she keeps up with the times and is very pleasant to be around. You know I love Ruthie with all my heart. She is like a sister to me. But, she is very stubborn and won't even go on a vacation with Ruth, although we know Ruth has asked her repeatedly to go to the Adirondacks or New England. Paul and Ruth are both brilliant and probably feel like being adventurous once in a while. I don't know what to think, dear," Billy said as he shrugged his shoulders.

"Maybe it truly is none of our business, and we should not say anything to Ruth—and, especially, Ruthie. It would break her heart. Maybe she knows about this, but I have a sick feeling she doesn't," said Cindy.

"I guess we should play it by ear until we see them this Sunday at church. If everything seems fine, we should assume this was a one-time, spontaneous fun session for Paul and Ruth. No harm in a little jitterbug or swing dance between friends. It wasn't like they were seen kissing. They were quite open about being together, now that I really think about it," Billy tried to reassure himself.

When they went to bed, Cindy and Billy fell asleep in each other's arms after telling one another how much they loved each other. They had been married for thirteen years and their cousin Ruth and Ruthie had lived together for fourteen. If something was wrong between their two best friends, they refused to let the same thing happen to their marriage.

CHAPTER THREE

Ruth's late afternoons with Paul had begun the very first Thursday of the new school year. Principal Slater wandered into her room about 3:30 and asked Ruth if she would accompany him to his newest hideout diner in Clayton, overlooking the St. Lawrence River. Ruth wasn't quite sure how she should respond.

"You know, Ruthie usually has dinner ready for me right at 5:30, so I think I must pass up this opportunity," Ruth replied with a smile.

"Well, I do think we could get you home by then if we leave right now for Dave's Fish 'n' Chips. Just an hour of your time would be appreciated, Ruth. My mind is in a dark place these days, and I need a true friend," Paul Slater pleaded.

With grave concern, Ruth looked at Paul and sensed much pain. She also knew this had nothing to do with her employment, given the recent glowing performance evaluation he had given her at the end of last school year. "If you put it that way, I think I can be a trusted friend. What are good colleagues for if not to discuss each other's problems?

It should only take us about fifteen minutes to drive there, you think? We'll drive separately and meet there. Okay?"

"Sounds good to me," Paul answered. With that, both were off to Clayton. All the way to Clayton, Ruth tried to imagine what had put Paul in such a dark mood. She had engaged in many social and political discussions with her boss and knew they seemed to think alike on most issues. They were both uncharacteristically liberal for the very conservative North Country.

Although it was never openly discussed, she knew Paul understood the true nature of her relationship with Ruthie, but seemed to have no problem with it. Paul was an Ivy Leaguer from Harvard. He was quite handsome, well-dressed, with impeccable manners. She always wondered why he had ended up in northern New York when his college degree from Harvard could have made the world his oyster. People at the church were always trying to throw the two of them together, because, from what Cindy told her, all these busybodies thought they would be an ideal couple. She had tired of their constant inquiries about "someone special in her life," to which she always replied that her father was the finest man she had ever known and until she found one as good as he, she would stay single. One woman at the church had even asked outright, "What about Paul Slater?" Ruth replied that it was never a good idea to date your boss, and that conversation ended quickly.

Cindy had once told Ruth that two women in the

Methodist Fellowship were very jealous of her because their husbands were always commenting on how good Ruth looked each Sunday. Cindy had joked to Ruth, "If only these poor women knew you are the last woman to become a homewrecker. Isn't it just amazing everyone tries to figure out why you aren't married? Yet, in your unique way, you are married every bit as much as Billy and me. Men have equipment you don't need to be passionately in love," Cindy chuckled.

Thank goodness for Cindy's confidential friendship, or Ruth believed she would have gone nuts long ago, pretending to the whole world to be someone she wasn't. As her thoughts concluded on her image in the Four Corners community, Ruth was in Clayton and pulled up to park behind Paul's car. When she walked into the Fish 'n' Chips, she saw Paul sitting in a booth overlooking the water. As she walked to the booth, she realized how smoky it was. There were several men sitting at the bar section of the diner puffing away on their cigarettes and cigars. She would have to think of some plan to get rid of that smell off her clothes before she got home. Ruthie discounted her own intelligence constantly, but the truth was that Ruth found Ruthie to be sharper than Sherlock Holmes, never failing to spot anything that might be amiss in her surroundings. This sleuthing ability had come in handy for the two women, because Ruthie never failed to pick up any signals from others that they might be on to the nature of their true relationship. Ruthie would make some comment in time to derail their interest. Maybe Ruthie didn't like engaging in debate as Ruth had at Smith, but Ruthie was every bit as quick on the uptake as Ruth.

"Well, this is a cozy little place, Paul, but a bit too smoky for my taste. I haven't been around too many smokers since college days, but I'll try to imagine myself back in one of those college hangouts," Ruth said.

"I appreciate that you were willing to meet me here, Ruth; you don't know how much. I've wanted to talk with you about other things than school for a long time, but I wanted to take some time to figure out if you could be my trusted friend who can keep secrets," Paul said.

"I believe I can be that sort of friend for you, Paul. What's on your mind? I was alarmed when you told me you were in a 'dark space,' as you called it," Ruth replied.

"Forgive me for intruding on your personal life, Ruth, and tell me if I am way off base here, but you and Ruthie are more than just friends, is that correct?" Paul asked.

Ruth measured her words carefully. "Would that be a problem for you if I am that type of woman?" She watched his face carefully as a kind smile illuminated his face, as she felt her heart pounding, awaiting his answer. This was her boss, and he could wreck her vocation just like that, if he wanted to. But she truly felt his kind smile might indicate he was not the sort of man to do that.

She was kept in suspense a bit longer as Paul got up from

the booth, wandered over to the jukebox, and dropped in a few quarters. The first song started playing before he got back to the booth—"My Girl" by the Temptations. Speaking in a hushed voice, Paul explained, "It would make me happy to know I am not the only queer in this town."

Ruth was rarely shocked about anything, but this revelation did come as a surprise. Yes, Paul was the best-dressed man in all of Four Corners, but she had been around gay men before in Provincetown when she was at Smith. He did not seem like any of the men she had met there. She attributed his impeccable dress and manners to his Harvard education and image. How had he ever ended up in Four Corners? Then she smiled, thinking, *How the hell did I end up here?*

Ruth finally recovered enough to say, "Rather a strange song for you to be playing on the jukebox if you are a man who is a little light in the loafers," Ruth laughed.

"I am playing it for you, so you can be thinking of Ruthie," Paul said. "Don't you do that with all the pop songs about love? Just apply them to your situation, even if you have to change a pronoun or two?"

"Of course I do," Ruth admitted.

"To tell you the truth, I am very jealous of your relationship with Ruthie. I wish I could have a partner myself. Despite all the community recognition you forego by hiding that love away, it still must be nice to go home to someone of a like orientation each night. Two women can always live together without much speculation. But substitute that scenario with two men, and you have a nightmare situation."

"Yes, I recognize it must be very difficult for you. To find anyone around these parts, and to date, and maybe even create a life with another man must be impossible," Ruth said. "Do you have anyone special in your life, Paul?"

"No, not really; I wish there were. I wake up every morning and ask myself Peggy Lee's old question, 'Is that all there is?' Is this my life forever?" Paul sat staring out the diner's large window overlooking the St. Lawrence River.

At long last, the bartender was at their booth and apologized for not inquiring as to their needs earlier. "My waitress is off tonight. What can I get you, Mr. Slater, and who is this fine-looking woman with you?" the bartender asked with a smile.

"Oh yes, allow me to introduce you to my vice principal, Ruth Packer. We needed to discuss some school issues away from prying minds and ears," Paul explained. "I have been so lacking in manners that I forgot to ask Miss Packer what she was drinking. Ruth, how about a drink? I'll have my usual."

Ruth looked about the bar and saw no one she knew. "Well, I am a good Methodist, but an enlightened one. Jesus didn't turn that water into Welch's grape juice, I am quite sure, so you can bring me some rosé. Drinking one glass of rosé probably will not send me to hell," Ruth laughed.

"Doubt you'll find many Methodists in here, Miss Packer. And, believe it or not, I've read the Bible, too. Didn't Saint Paul say, 'Take a little wine for thy stomach's sake'?" The bartender winked at Ruth and headed to the bar for their drinks. He was back in a flash with their liquid refreshment, and the private conversation between Ruth and Paul continued.

"I guess you are the wise, witty, and sophisticated woman I had assessed you to be. Ruth, if I could count on your confidentiality and friendship, and an occasional after-school drink or dinner, I might be able to survive for a couple more years in this backwater. These people around here are ignorant of the fact that people like us even exist. In some ways, that's good, because they assume I should marry you. Don't get me wrong. If we were the people they assume we are, you would be the first woman I would ask to marry. You are pretty, you know, and truly the smartest woman I have ever met," Paul said just before taking another drink of his scotch.

Ruth was still perplexed about how to handle Paul's request for friendship. She needed to be clear with Paul that she was not interested in becoming his pretend girlfriend to defer gossip in the community about why he remained a bachelor. Ruthie would be hurt and angry if this subterfuge were even attempted. On the other hand, she did enjoy talking with a very intelligent man who was so kind. After taking the first drink of her rosé and realizing how good it tasted, she looked directly into Paul's eyes and said, "I like you very much, and I want to be your friend. I think it would be very cathartic for both of us. I am just not willing to be your pretend girlfriend for the community's benefit. That would not be fair to Ruthie, and I will do anything to save her from hurt," Ruth said.

"Oh, Ruth, I am not asking you to cut Ruthie out of the picture at all. In fact, you can tell her all about me and maybe, if she wants, the three of us can get together occasionally," Paul suggested.

"No, I don't think it would be good to either tell Ruthie about you, our 'conferences,' or suggesting we all go out to dinner. Two is company and three is a crowd as they say, and Ruthie can get quite jealous of my time with others. She is so needy in that department, and it is something I need to take up with her soon because it is driving me nuts. Until we get that issue resolved, better to just sneak over here once a week for a quick chat where no one is likely to see us. I don't worry about what townsfolk would say. They'd probably smile and say, 'It is about time those two got together,' but if such gossip got back to Ruthie, she'd be devastated."

And so began the weekly "conferences" between Paul and Ruth. Any Monday through Thursday night, they would drive off to Clayton for an hour or hour and a half.

They never went on Friday nights because Clayton was too full of people, and Paul had started weekend trips to Syracuse, seldom getting back for church. People at the church speculated he had a girlfriend in Syracuse. Paul had just secured a boyfriend in Syracuse, Robert Wellington, who was an associate professor of art history. Ruth was very happy for Paul and really enjoyed their chats, as Paul regaled her with stories of "walking on the wild side" in Syracuse. The wild side group was quite small, but there were a few men who got together for weekend house parties. When they were not discussing his new romance, Paul and Ruth discussed the fast-moving events of the 1960s. The war in Viet Nam was raging, the civil rights movement was exploding, and their students were beginning to experiment with long hair and mini-skirts, although the latter was something Ruth had to reluctantly discuss with the girls who attempted to wear them.

Ruth started to enjoy her late afternoons with Paul. She believed that, next to Ruthie, Paul could become her best friend. Feeling free to talk about her whole life, with someone who knew what it was like to always be hiding part of your life away from others, was cathartic. In addition, Paul was brilliant, handsome, and kind, with impeccable manners. He was the "whole package," as people sometimes said these days in describing the perfect man.

Upon their sixth return to Dave's Fish 'n' Chips on October 13, they both put a couple quarters in the jukebox and talked about their favorite music. Both had grown up in the swing era but agreed Elvis Presley had a wonderful voice and that the Beatles were interesting.

"Do you like to dance?" Paul inquired.

Ruth smiled and thought about the private dance lessons she had given Ruthie when they first became a couple. Unless there was a church event, they had a standing date to dance every Saturday evening on their hardwood floor dining room. Ruth would put on an album of big band tunes, Ruthie would make sure the drapes were drawn, and they would dance across the living room floor for at least an hour. Ruthie became a very good dancer, despite her protestations to the contrary. This continued for a few years, and then, like everything else, somehow, they let the dancing fade out of their Saturday evenings, which were now usually spent in front of the TV.

"Actually, I do like to dance," Ruth said. "It has been years since I was on the dance floor, so I believe I am pretty rusty now."

"Well, let's find out," Paul said in a challenging tone.

"Right here?" Ruth replied.

"Sure, right here. I've seen plenty of teenagers jitterbugging right in front of that jukebox," Paul explained. "No one will mind. But maybe you are too shy or too proud to do it," Paul challenged. Just at that point "Blue Suede Shoes" started playing. With that, Ruth bounded off her side of the booth, telling Paul that she'd give him "a run for his money."

And so, they were off and flying about the floor, jitterbugging their hearts out. At one point they both shed their suit jackets and continued dancing. When "In the Mood" played next, Paul took Ruth securely in hand, and they elegantly waltzed from one end of the room to the other, as the patrons clapped for them. When they sat back down in their booth, the bartender brought over two fresh drinks and told them, "They're on the house. I haven't seen marvelous dancing like that in ages. Maybe you two should try to dance on *The Lawrence Welk Show*," he suggested.

Ruth and Paul looked at one another and then exploded into laughter. They did make great dance partners, but that was as far as their partnership would ever go. How nice it felt to dance out in public like this, they both admitted quietly to one another after the bartender left their booth. The dancing seemed to chase the worries of the day away, until Ruth looked at the clock and saw it was 6:15! Ruth quietly whispered in Paul's ear that Ruthie was going to kill her for being so late. Ruth ran out the door and into her car before Paul could say anything.

CHAPTER FOUR

Sunday, October 16, 1966

Sunday arrived, and the four friends greeted one another just outside the sanctuary door. Billy thought Ruthie seemed a little down in the mouth and invited her, as usual, to sit next to him and his family in the same pew. Ruth ran off to perform her piano-playing duties. "You feel okay this morning, Ruthie?" Billy inquired as he arranged his children between himself and Cindy in the pew.

"Actually, I'm feeling pretty arthritic today. This cold and damp weather really makes my joints hurt, especially, in the places where my body hit that darn barn floor two years ago. I'm feeling very old today, Billy. Hopefully the sermon and service will take my mind off my pain," Ruthie said as a slight smile appeared on her face for the first time.

Billy took his old chum's hand and said, "I think about that horrible day you fell, and I realize how lucky we all were to have found you alive. This would be a sad little hamlet without you around, Ruthie." He squeezed Ruthie's hand.

"Don't think you are right about that, Billy. Everyone is replaceable. The older you get, the more you realize just how dispensable you are," Ruthie said, as she scanned the Sunday bulletin. Billy glanced over toward Cindy, who had a sad expression on her face after overhearing his conversation with Ruthie.

The text from the Gospel that morning was from the "Sermon on the Mount." Pastor Hutchinson was a fine sermonizer. He always had an interesting story that you would remember long into the coming week. Four Corners was extraordinarily lucky to have him as their pastor for so many years, given the Methodist Church's habit of moving pastors about the Conference every five years.

"As I just read to you, Jesus made it very clear that we should not judge others for their sins of commission or omission because we, too, from time to time fall short of the glory of God due to our own iniquities. But what does this really mean when we know for sure that a friend has gone astray and is, perhaps, in danger of causing themselves, or someone else, irreparable harm if they don't stop sinning? Do we say nothing? Do we just pray for that person and ask God to set their feet on the right path? If we love our brothers and sisters as Jesus commands we do, is there no intervention on our part if we clearly know that they are destroying their own life by their conduct?

"My second year in seminary, I had the eye-opening experience of helping out in the Bowery Mission soup kitchen in New York City.The Bowery was in a section of New York City, which had fallen, economically, from being a wealthy, well-regarded area of the city, into depravity, as drunks, drug addicts and prostitutes roamed the streets trying to survive any way they could. Into this oblivion, the Bowery Mission arose in the late 1800s to feed the hungry, provide an occasional bed for the homeless, and offer an alternative to homelessness by getting people treatment for their particular addiction, as well as helping these lost souls find a job, which would make them feel their lives had meaning and purpose. We were instructed by the mission administrator not to evangelize, or judge behavior until we were sure he, and sometimes she, had been physically fed and was sober.

"One of the first men I met that first day at the mission, was a middle-aged fellow who looked as if he had been on the street for weeks. His clothes were filthy, his hair oily as well as dirty, and he smelled bad, with a strong odor of alcohol. I must admit I was even uncomfortable to shake his hand as he came in the door. However, I did extend my hand to him and, just as I did, he vomited all over me. I recoiled in horror and without thinking yelled, 'How disgusting. You'd think you would get yourself sober before daring to come through this door!' With that having been shouted out to all in the mission, he turned around and ran out the door as fast as he could. I stood there for several seconds trying to figure out what to do next. I then made a hasty retreat to the restroom to clean myself off as best I could and then headed out onto the streets to try and find him, but to no avail.

"I didn't sleep very well that night in my seminary dorm room, or for several more nights after that. On the last night of my sleeplessness, I suddenly remembered a night when I was in college, but still living at home, when I went out with some boys for an evening on the town. I experimented with beer for the first time in my life while wolfing down some hot dogs. By the time I got home at 1 a.m., things were spinning around in my head, and as I tried to climb up the stairs, I got sick all over the stairs."

All the congregation could hear Mrs. Sawyer, the president of the Women's Christian Temperance Union, gasp loudly from hearing her Methodist pastor making such an admission of drunken behavior. Ruthie grabbed Billy's hand as she tried to stifle her laugh.

Unfazed by Mrs. Sawyer's gasp, their brave pastor continued his story. "My teetotaling Methodist mother had heard my vomiting and was by my side trying to help me up the stairs. She told me to clean myself off and go to bed. We would talk in the morning. There was no doubt in my mind she knew I was drunk, but she was wise enough to know that it was best for us to talk about why and how this had happened when I would be in a better place to explain myself.

"Judge not, lest you be judged," Pastor Hutchinson

repeated as he looked over the faces of the congregation. The congregation was completely silent, with their full attention drawn to their spiritual leader. The pastor continued, "How was I any different than the man I turned away from the mission that day by my judgmental ravings? I had gotten just as drunk as he. There was one big difference—my loving mom, who took me in her arms and helped me get into a warm bed, without saying a word. The man at the mission didn't have that mother in his life then to help him out, and perhaps he never did.

"And herein lies the meaning of Christ's admonition to 'judge not, lest you be judged.' Often, we judge people for the very sins we are afraid to admit we have also committed, or we have overlooked another sin in our life that is just as bad, if not worse, than the sin of the man at the Bowery Mission, or the biblical account of the woman at the well. Jesus teaches us to reach out to others no matter the sin, because we are no better. Once we are kind and loving to those in trouble because of their sin, and we have helped them as best we can, we will be approaching that unconditional love and humility God is willing to bestow upon all. Others will see and feel our love, which comes from God, and ask us how they, too, may obtain it."

Pastor Hutchinson stared out over the congregation for a few moments and then sat down as Ruth played, "Just as I Am." Billy and Cindy looked at one another and raised their eyebrows as they stood to sing the hymn. On the way home, Cindy was the first to comment on the sermon. "If that sermon wasn't perfect for today, then I don't know what sermon would be. It's kind of eerie, don't you think? It is almost as if you or John phoned Rev. Hutchinson this week and ordered a sermon on this topic," Cindy said.

Their eldest child spoke up from the back seat. "Has Uncle Johnny been sinning, Mom?"

"We forget about those astute little twelve-year-old ears, don't we, Mom?"

Billy laughed and then addressed his child. "No. Actually your Uncle John is one of the best men I know. We all commit sins from time to time. Today's sermon really tells us we should remember we are not perfect before we start criticizing other's bad behavior."

Billy continued, "The thing I like best about our pastor is that he is unafraid to put his own sins into one of his sermons. He tells us personal stories from his life and takes some risk doing so from time to time. I keep thinking about Mrs. Sawyer's loud gasp as she heard that her own pastor had gotten drunk to the point of vomiting when he was planning to be a minister of the Gospel. That woman is such a prude; I am not at all surprised she is truly an old maid. Did you see how Ruthie grabbed my hand and was squeezing it hard to keep herself from laughing out loud? Why, Ruthie's face was turning beet red after that gasp," Billy laughed.

After the Sunday dinner, the kids ran outside to play

in the leaves. As usual, Cindy and Billy sat at their kitchen table and watched the children play, through the picture window, and lingered over their coffee. Finally, Cindy spoke. "You know I've been good friends with both Ruth and Ruthie individually. I truly can't say I prefer one of them over the other. When you are around Ruthie, you feel like she's been your friend forever, and would be your friend no matter how disappointing you might turn out to be to her sometime. You feel safe, at home, no pretenses about Ruthie. I see why you wanted her to be your wife, I really do. Now, Ruth is no less of a person than Ruthie, although very different. Perhaps because she went to Smith, she is worldlier or, at the very least, a little more cosmopolitan. She is more adventurous, from what I've seen on our shopping trips, and willing to try new things," Cindy said

Billy quickly chimed in, "Would that adventurousness include trying a new thing like dating Paul Slater?" Billy asked.

"You see, that's a conundrum for me. I don't know. Most everyone else in Four Corners would think that's what Ruth's doing, and Lord help us should Four Corners Methodist Church think otherwise. And maybe, just maybe, Ruth is tired of going against the grain of society and wants to experience what it would be like to have a normal social life, which she and Ruthie do not," Cindy said.

"Well, if that is the case, she better be honest with Ruthie. I know Ruth is my cousin, but Ruthie is like a sister to me now, and I don't want her hurt under any circumstances," Billy said, in an unusually harsh tone.

"I'm going to whip up a special type of sticky buns, call Ruthie, and see if she's up for coffee tomorrow morning. You know, I heard after church today that Arnold Jackson is stepping down as accountant and treasurer of the dairy co-operative at the end of the year. Maybe I can convince Ruthie she ought to put her name out there as a possible replacement. That's a genuinely fine reason to pop by and quietly inquire about how things are on the home front. No offense, but I think she is more likely to open up to me than to you," Cindy said.

CHAPTER FIVE

Cindy pulled into the driveway about 9 a.m. and wasted no time in grabbing her sticky buns from the passenger seat and dashing off to the side door of Ruthie's home. She had called at 7:30 a.m. to inquire if Ruthie wanted to have coffee. Ruthie always enjoyed these morning get-togethers. Once Cindy and Ruthie were settled at the kitchen table with coffee and a sticky bun, Cindy began her first task. "Ruthie, did you hear that Arnold Jackson is retiring as the cooperative's bookkeeper and treasurer at the end of the year?"

"As a matter of fact, Billy mentioned to me a few weeks back that Arnold was thinking about retiring. He will be missed. The Stein family was the benefit of his honesty in measuring the weight of milk from our farm, and my dad always enjoyed chatting with him," Ruthie said.

"Why don't you put your name out there to take his place?" Cindy inquired. "I understand they pay a decent wage of $3.75 an hour. All the farmers know you, and you kept the milk records of the Stein farm from the time you graduated from high school until you stopped milking in

1964. Billy told me you taught him how to keep the books for the Packer farm and that your own records were impeccable. I should think the cooperative would hire you right away," Cindy enthused.

"I am not sure I would be the kind of treasurer and bookkeeper they are looking for," Ruthie said. "I have no formal bookkeeping training, and no woman has ever held that position."

"And no woman that I know of in all of Upstate New York has taken over a dairy farming operation all by herself and made it profitable. More reason for you to apply. Things are slowly changing. We never had a woman vice principal before, and look at Ruth! Times are changing, and all the men in the cooperative have not forgotten you were the top high school student, as well as a Regent's diploma recipient. You can pick up anything just like that," Cindy replied, as she snapped her fingers for emphasis. "You must be bored stiff by now hanging around the house most days. As nice as it may be for Ruth, you don't have to do the cooking every night," Cindy said. "You'd have your weekends with Ruth, since it is a Monday through Friday office job. You don't have to cook for Ruth every night."

"That is certainly true enough now. Ruth is often so late coming home from school these days that I find it difficult to keep the food hot for her," Ruthie scoffed.

"Really? Thought you two always ate right at 5:30?" Cindy said.

"I thought that time had been fixed a long time ago myself," Ruthie replied. "However, since this new school term began, she has been late at least once a week. She could have the decency to at least call me and let me know she'll be late. I realize being a vice principal sometimes requires conferences after school with parents, or mandatory faculty meetings. She used to let me know in the morning or call me during the day and tell me about these things. No longer! Is this what naturally happens after fourteen years?" Ruthie said.

Cindy was now more suspicious than ever that Ruth was keeping something unsavory from Ruthie. Yet she was not quite sure she was ready to tell Ruthie what she knew about Ruth's latest tardiness. She had said a prayer on the way over that God would give her direction and discernment in this conversation. Before she revealed anything she knew about this situation, she would gently pry a bit more.

"You must know better than I, Ruthie, that after thirteen or fourteen years of being together, partners can sometimes take each other for granted. We shouldn't do that, but we do. Billy and I take each other for granted frequently. There have been times I was late getting home to make dinner after a shopping trip into Watertown, or a Methodist Women's event. He knows I love to window shop, and after church meetings I sometimes chat too long with other women. In both cases, I lose track of time. He can get irritated with me about a later- than-usual dinner because he's ready for a big supper after all that heavy work. But, fortunately, as you know, Ruthie, Billy is easygoing and has enough patience for both of us. We usually get it all worked out after we sit down and talk about our upset," Cindy said.

"Yes, I should be more like Billy and realize my partner needs to have some breathing room. It's just that I love Ruth and need her so much that when she is late coming home, I envision her in some ditch by the side of the road, and I'm not there to help her," Ruthie admitted.

"Well, have the two of you tried to talk through this recent tardiness issue?" Cindy asked.

"Not in the way we should, I guess. Last Thursday, when she was late by almost an hour and a half, I verbally flew at her like a banshee, as soon as she walked in the door, demanding an explanation for being so late," Ruthie confessed. "After that, any possibility of us reasonably discussing the issue all went downhill."

Cindy was now on the edge of her seat, blurting out, "And just what was her explanation?"

"That woman is too clever with arguments. She turned the issue right around on me and reminded me of all the times dinner was late when we were on the farm and some farm emergency delayed our dinner. She went on, in a hurtful voice, saying that I should trust her by now, and she gave no explanation," Ruthie recounted.

"That doesn't sound like the cousin Ruth I know. Oh, don't get me wrong. I believe every word you are telling me.

Do you suppose it could just be forgetfulness as to the time she was leaving school to come home? The change of life with all its hormonal instability, causes some middle-aged women to do some unexplainable things sometimes? She is forty-two, and some women go through menopause earlier than others," Cindy suggested.

"Could be," Ruthie said. "I know she seems more distracted and fatigued this fall. She has always been such an energetic woman; it is strange to see her eat her dinner, watch the nightly news with me, and then head right off to bed. By the time I take AJ outside for a minute or two, turn off all the lights, and lock the doors, when I walk into the bedroom she is always asleep," Ruthie said.

Cindy could hear the disappointment in Ruthie's voice. Why wouldn't Ruth be exhausted at night, if she was frequently dancing her feet off, like a teenager, with Paul Slater during the work week. She had never discussed Ruth and Ruthie's intimacy with either of them, but until this morning she thought nothing was amiss in the love department.

Cindy finally responded, after a long sip of coffee. "Well, I think you need to sit down with Ruth and tell her how you are feeling lonely for the old Ruth. I know Billy and I discuss many family matters and community concerns each night when we go to bed. I look forward to those discussions, and I know I'd be upset if he was already asleep every night I got into bed.

"As your friend, I'd suggest you not let this issue between you and Ruth fester. I also want you to get on the phone tomorrow with the cooperative president and tell him of your interest in Arnold's job when he retires in December. Billy would be thrilled to have you take over that position. You could, no doubt, get in a good twenty years of work and accrue a nice little pension. You'd feel really good about yourself, and there would be no waiting around for Ruth to come home," Cindy said. She knew what she was going to do next about this Paul Slater situation. She'd ask Ruth if she wanted to go shopping for clothes this Saturday, and while they were driving to Watertown, she'd just confront Ruth with John's observations in Clayton.

All the way home, Cindy replayed the conversation with Ruthie. She heard an edge in Ruthie's voice, along with unhappiness that was different from the depression Ruthie had experienced after her fall in the barn two years ago. It was so sad to hear Ruthie objectify Ruth as "that woman" when she discussed Ruth's maddening ability to have an answer for everything.

Cindy's mother had taught her as a teenager never to get involved in trying to fix someone else's relationship. Her mother had emphasized that no good could come of it, and people would resent her for inserting herself into their problems. However wise her mother was about many things, how could she let these two special women destroy fourteen years of life together?

Billy was not going to wait for Cindy to get a full explanation from Ruth about what was going on with Paul Slater. He knew the bartender, Clifford Carpenter, who had graduated with him and Ruthie. He hadn't really talked to Clifford in years, but he knew Clifford to be a very friendly guy who would be happy to see an old classmate. Billy told John it was John's night to do the evening chores with their hired hand, as Billy planned to make a run into Clayton. John raised his eyebrows and observed, "You think that is wise? What if you run into our cousin, Ruth? Wouldn't it be uncomfortable for you both?"

"Well, it might be uncomfortable for Ruth if anything serious is going on, but better for Ruthie that I find out about it first! Isn't this just crazy, John? Anyone else in Four Corners who saw Paul and Ruth together would say, 'How nice. It's about time.'" But for us, Ruth's actions might well result in a broken heart for Ruthie, and we don't want that to happen."

All the way to Clayton, Billy kept thinking about Ruthie. He still loved her very much, as if she were his sister, and would always be protective of her heart. He knew Ruthie had always felt socially awkward and that this awkwardness had been further amplified by her mother's unkind remarks about Ruthie not being feminine enough. He had no idea what caused women to love women or men to love men. If it had anything to do with the lack of a good mother-daughter relationship for women, it was no wonder Ruthie wanted to be held in the arms of a kind, attractive woman, because Ruthie's mother had not given her daughter the love and respect she was due. He was happy that his cousin had waltzed into Ruthie's heart, but now, after fourteen years, was that all coming apart?

He wasted no time in getting to Dave's Fish 'n' Chips, and found his old high school friend, Clifford, behind the bar. Clifford was happy to see Billy, and they exchanged pleasantries about their respective families. While Billy turned down the beer Clifford wanted to give him, he did order a burger basket and a Coke. Billy began his investigation. "So, I suppose your quietest time here is on the weekday afternoons?"

"Generally, that is true, but once in a while on a weekday, this place can get rockin', as they say," Clifford said.

"Looks pretty quiet around here this afternoon. When's the last time this place was jumping?" Billy casually asked, as he dunked one of his fries into some ketchup.

"Well, about two weeks ago, we had a distinguished-looking couple dancing like they were on American Bandstand. They were so good that the patrons were clapping and cheering them on loudly, and people were coming in off the street to see what was going on. I monetarily cleaned up that afternoon, making the most money I ever made on an off-season weekday. In the summer, we stay busy from all the tourists, as you know, but in the late fall and winter months it is dead here, except for a handful of locals who make this an afternoon stop before calling it a day," Clifford said.

"You say this was a 'distinguished-looking couple.' Who do we have around these parts who is distinguished-looking?" Billy laughed.

"One of them I know quite well. He's the school district principal from Four Corners, Paul Slater. He started coming here about two years ago, every other day or so, after school. Heck of a nice guy, and always impeccably dressed in his suit. I think he just likes to unwind and have a scotch or two once in a while. He seemed lonely to me until about six weeks ago when he started meeting this good-looking woman here. She was 'dressed to the nines,' as they say, and ever so nice and witty. She was very down-to-earth and not snooty at all. I'd love to date her myself. It is the happiest I have seen Paul Slater in the two years he's been coming here," Clifford said.

"So, their dancing was really that spectacular?" Billy asked, as he slurped the last of his Coke through the straw.

"Oh yes. Never seen anything like it. It was almost like they had just graduated from an Arthur Murray studio or something. And they were having ever so much fun. The other patrons could see they really enjoyed each other, something nice to see from a couple in their late thirties or early forties. You usually only see that enthusiasm from the kids that go to Paul's school," Clifford said with a big smile.

"You had never seen that woman before?" Billy asked.

"No, but I am trying to recall her first name because Paul introduced her to me the first time they met here. Let me see, her name was Rose, or Rosie, or—oh, I know, her name was Ruth. He told me she was the vice principal of his school. I didn't see any ring on her finger, so I assume she must be divorced, or the men of this world are letting a classy dame slip right through their fingers all these years. I thought, at the time, good for Paul. He's a nice guy and she was a nice woman. They just seemed perfect for one another. You don't always see that, you know," Clifford said.

"No, that is quite true. Couples sometimes get mismatched and don't discover how much different they are from one another until years later. Around these parts, once you've figured out you are with the wrong spouse, you usually just put up with the inconvenience, knowing how divorce is frowned upon still. I am glad I am so happy with my Cindy," Billy said as he slapped a five-dollar bill on the counter and remarked to Clifford his burger basket was delicious. "So just keep the change, my friend."

Driving back to the farm, he felt woefully disappointed in his cousin, Ruth. It was obvious this little dance episode had occurred after she and Paul had been at the diner on several occasions before. As he pictured the two of them together, he could see what an attractive couple they made. Ruth had always been the fun-loving cousin in his family, finding a way to get everyone laughing and enjoying themselves, even at the dullest family reunions. He admitted to himself that his dear Ruthie, with a heart of gold, was bland in comparison.

When it had been confirmed to him by Ruth two years ago, after Ruthie's dreadful accident in the barn, that the two of them were lovers, he had hoped that maybe his cousin would bring some real joy into Ruthie's life and help loosen up the always serious Ruthie. But as the years were moving on, he believed their relationship was the same, minus all the passion he had sensed in them when they first moved in together. Maybe it was not right for him to be imposing his idea of a marriage upon a lesbian relationship. He was out of his element in this situation, and only his beloved Cindy would know what to think.

When he walked into the farmhouse, Cindy could see he was upset. "John tells me you wandered into Clayton today to see your old classmate, Clifford. Did you end up going to Clifford's diner?" Cindy inquired.

"Yes, I did, and I really wish I hadn't," Billy lamented. "To tell you the truth, I just want to stay right out of all this controversy. I don't know what to think about the situation with Ruth and Paul. It seems like something intense is going on between them. Clifford said they had been meeting at the diner for about six weeks. He had nothing but praise for both and went on and on about how Ruth made Paul so happy, and how witty and wonderful Ruth was in talking with Clifford. He said he wished he could marry Ruth himself, that she was apparently a pearl that had been unnoticed by all of mankind until now. It made me so uncomfortable to hear all this and realize his observations were no doubt 100% true," Billy said.

"Did he say anything about them holding hands, or even kissing, and did they always arrive in separate cars?" Cindy wanted to know.

"I didn't get that detailed with my questions. I thought I would sound like a private detective, or an agent for the CIA or something. If they were into torrid displays of public affection, he would have said that. Knowing my cousin she would never publicly engage in that blatant type of behavior," Billy said, as he hung his head in his hands.

Cindy put her arms around Billy as he sat in his chair staring at the cup of coffee she had just delivered. "Look, Billy, don't get so downcast about all this. I know you love Ruthie, and you greatly admire your cousin. Even if the worst is happening for their relationship right now, it is not your fault, and you should not be concentrating on the tragedy of the whole mess. We were right to help them stay together and support their companionship for the past fourteen years. Remember how ecstatic Ruthie was after six months of living with Ruth? Remember how Ruthie took Ruth in at a time when Ruth really had nothing but a diploma? Remember how Ruth stuck by Ruthie after Ruthie fell and had no problem about being the main provider for the two of them for the rest of their lives? Remember how sweetly they used to smile at one another when we were over at their house playing cards, the special twinkle in their eyes when their eyes met? We always talked about those things as we drove home from their house and thought that God surely must have had a hand in getting them together.

"So, my dear, if nothing else, we have helped them have fourteen wonderful years together in a part of rural America where companions for them would be almost impossible to find. As I review all these factors with you, I am thinking that maybe Ruth, particularly, needs to be reminded of all the goodness she and Ruthie have experienced together. Maybe it is not all over for them. We need to ask God to help us properly help them. There is no one else who can reach out to them. But before I intercede any further in this relationship, I need to talk with Ruth and place it right on the line for her," Cindy said.

CHAPTER SIX

Just as Cindy had hoped, Ruth agreed to take a trip into Watertown with her for some winter clothing and to have lunch at the Crystal restaurant. Cindy picked up Ruth at her home, just as Ruthie was all dressed up and headed out the door to the cooperative to discuss her interest in the upcoming bookkeeping job.

"My goodness, Ruthie, don't you look swell in that pants outfit," Cindy remarked. "That red sweater with that gray suit is a perfect color for you—don't you think, Ruth?" Cindy said.

"Ruth should know, I guess, because she's the one who picked out this outfit for me today. She's the one with impeccable taste," Ruthie said, as she passed by both women on the way to her car.

"Well, of course she has impeccable taste. She picked you, didn't she?" Cindy shouted out happily.

"And the older I get, the more I worry about her judgment in that department," Ruthie replied, as she slid behind the wheel of her car and closed the door.

"You've just witnessed the type of comments coming

out of Ruthie's mouth these days that demonstrate she has no self-esteem or confidence that she is a wonderful woman, inside and out," Ruth said, as they climbed into Cindy's car and headed down Route 12 to Watertown.

Cindy was exploding with curiosity about what was really going on with Ruth, and she knew if she waited any longer she wouldn't have the courage to ask. "Ruth, you know, next to Billy, you are my best friend and that we don't keep secrets from one another, right? And you also know that whatever we discuss between ourselves stays with us, unless we give permission to have it shared even with our spouses?"

"Of course, I know that, Cindy," Ruth said, with concern in her voice. "Why are you being so serious? What's up?" Ruth asked.

"There is no good way to explain this but just come right out with it. A week ago this past Thursday, Billy sent John into Clayton to run an errand in late afternoon." As soon as these first words came from Cindy, Ruth was feeling dread as to what she would hear next and how she would explain herself.

"Billy always encourages John to take his time and have a burger or something, so he can get away from Alice for a few hours. You surely can understand that. Anyway, he decided to try out Dave's Fish 'n' Chips, and when he went into the diner, he saw . . . ."

"Let me stop you right there, Cindy. John saw me dancing

with Paul Slater, and all the patrons were clapping as we danced to 'Blue Suede Shoes' and 'In the Mood,'" Ruth said.

"Well, yes, that is exactly what he said. He told Billy, and Billy told me about what John had seen. No one else in Four Corners knows about this as far as I know, and even if they did, I suppose the only thing old-time Methodists might be surprised at is the fact you were dancing in a bar right after school hours. Otherwise, it would seem logical and sweet that you and Paul were hitting it off. But what concerns me is that, apparently, Ruthie knows nothing about this, and I don't want Ruthie to get unnecessarily hurt by hearing about it from anyone but you. I really do understand how you and Paul Slater could be very attracted to one another and how much easier it would be for you to be in a relationship with him. The two of you make the perfect couple. You both are good-looking and brilliant, with Ivy League-level educations. You told me about dating men when you lived in Cooperstown, and while I'm no Masters and Johnson, I know there are some women who have been with both men and women. I'd just ask you to be honest with Ruthie about this and not have her hear about this from the next person who wanders into Clayton in the late afternoon," Cindy said.

"Wow! You believe I am cheating on Ruthie, don't you?" Ruth responded in a very quiet voice, blankly staring out the window as the car moved through the farms on Route 12. "I guess I was fooling myself that there was any place near Four Corners where I could confidentially meet with a friend for an hour or so, without someone seeing me and getting a wrong impression of what I am doing. I am hurt, as well, that you could think I would have an intimate relationship with anyone but Ruthie," Ruth said.

"Well, what are you doing, Ruth? Explain exactly what is going on with Paul Slater, so that I can understand. You know I will not even speak of this to Billy if you ask me to keep it private between us. I mean, what was John to think when he saw you that Thursday evening? Billy was so upset, he went to the diner to find out if you had been there before. The bartender graduated with Billy and Ruthie, so he just went in, had a burger, and hinted around about any unusual happenings at Dave's Fish 'n' Chips. He's told that you and Paul were all the rage dancing that night, and you had been there with Paul at least five or six times before," Cindy said, in the least judgmental tone she could muster.

"First, whether you want to believe me or not—and I hope you know me well enough after our fourteen years of friendship to believe me—there is nothing going on between Paul and myself except pure friendship. Our going to Clayton after school about once a week just started this school term, upon his invitation. I went the first time after initially saying no, because he admitted he was struggling with depression and wanted someone he thought he could trust to discuss his depression," Ruth explained

"Well, I guess you must be a miracle worker to get him

up and dancing about like you two were just at the malt shop, listening to the jukebox. I can't say that sounds like a depressed man to me," Cindy replied sarcastically.

Ruth was angry. She didn't know if she was angry at Cindy for her last comment, or angrier at herself for being so stupid as to agree to these Clayton "conferences" for the past six weeks. She would not disclose that Paul was gay, for that was really nothing Cindy needed to know, and she had promised complete confidentiality to Paul. This was something she knew she needed to sort out for herself, which would logically mean Ruthie knowing about the reason for her tardiness at dinner the last few weeks.

"You are very quiet, Ruth. You sure there isn't more to this story that you are not telling me? Maybe it is none of my business?" Cindy said in a timid voice.

"Look, Cindy, all I can tell you is the God's truth. I am not intimately involved with Paul Slater in any way. I won't lie. I do enjoy getting together with him once a week for an hour or so to talk about what's going on at school, in the world, and how he might address his depression situation. But he clearly knows we will never be more than just friends. He knows Ruthie and I are lifetime companions and has no problem with it. He has known that for some time and has promised he will never violate confidentiality about that part of my life, just as I have promised to him that I will not tell anyone about the source of his depression. You think I haven't noticed he is very handsome, debonair, and brilliant? Of course I have, and that makes him very fun to be around. You think I enjoyed our one dancing escapade? I most certainly did. How wonderful it was to dance out in public like that with someone who also grew up with ballroom dancing lessons before he went to Harvard. I felt so free that night, dancing like a madwoman, and all the way home I thought what a wonderful thing it would be if Ruthie and I could dance like that in public, with people clapping and shouting. But if Ruthie and I danced like that in public, we would be ridden out of town on a rail, and it would be said, 'How dare those dykes dance like that out in front of God and everybody,'" Ruth emphatically stated.

Cindy really wanted to believe this woman who had never lied to her before, but she also realized Ruth might be honestly needing a new kind of life she could not have with Ruthie. Before she could think of what to say next, Ruth continued her explanation.

"Ruthie and I may have had our adjustment problems over these last fourteen years, but I have never cheated on her. Do you know what I thought when Ruthie and I became lovers? I was astounded that a woman of her character and passion existed, and I knew God had put her in my life forever. I still remember, clearly, the feeling of completion when Ruthie first took me in her strong arms and gently made love to me. I knew right then I never wanted to have a male suitor and certainly not a husband. I haven't forgotten that it was Ruthie who first gave me a home when I had nothing but educational potential that no one seemed to need. I remember, still, the horror of thinking how I easily could have lost her when she took that terrible fall in the barn, and how much I wanted to take care of her now that my teaching career was finally on track again." Tears started streaming down Ruth's cheeks as she reached into her purse for a handkerchief. "So, don't you ever doubt my love for Ruthie, Cindy. It cuts me right to the heart that you would ever think I would cheat on her. We are going through a really rough time right now, but give me a chance to make this right with Ruthie before you give up on me," Ruth said.

Cindy felt terrible about making her good friend cry. She had no reason to doubt the sincerity of Ruth's tears. Ruth was not a crier normally, and Cindy felt badly about insinuating infidelity to Ruthie. She reached across the car and placed her hand on Ruth's shoulder. "I believe everything you have told me. I still don't completely understand why you haven't told Ruthie about your friendship with Paul. Why did you keep this from her?" Cindy asked.

"Okay, I can see why this seems inscrutable to you. Now, I need your guarantee that this conversation will not go out of this car. Ruthie gets insanely jealous about any time I spend with anyone outside church members and your family. I really don't think she believes I would cheat on her. That fear was laid aside a couple years ago when another woman, whom I haven't told you about, tried to insert herself into our relationship right after Ruthie's fall. Ruthie saw how I made it very clear to this woman that there was only one woman who would ever be allowed to hold me in her arms as a lover, and that woman was Ruthie.

"However, Ruthie wants all my time and attention, and I am beginning to feel smothered. A mature relationship recognizes that each partner has needs the other partner will never be able to meet. I am an extrovert. I need lots of quality people in my life as friends and acquaintances. Ruthie is an introvert. She wants to keep to herself and have me right beside her all the time. I am now midway or more through my life, and I want to get out of our cave and do things, such as traveling about the state, maybe New England. We can afford it, but Ruthie always comes up with some reason not to go on vacation. I really look forward to our pinochle nights with you and Billy, and I hope they continue for as long as we can hold cards in our hands. But Ruthie and I need more exploration of the world together. We need to be doing that now, before we are both too decrepit to go anywhere. Can you understand what I am trying to tell you, Cindy?" Ruth asked.

"Yes, I certainly see your point. Things can get dull in a relationship if you are just doing the same exact thing year in and year out. To some extent, I guess I am more like you, and Billy is more like Ruthie. He doesn't see the need to travel beyond Four Corners although he is outgoing and gregarious, so our social circles here are many, which will never be the case with Ruthie," Cindy admitted.

"I've made a point of keeping any complaints about Ruthie from you, because I know I am not perfect either, and I probably fail at some level to be a good partner to her," Ruth said. "I do love Ruthie, but I want our relationship to flourish and bloom. I want us to try and recapture at least some of that passion we both felt in those first days as lovers. I don't want to think that is impossible. Sometimes I will lie in bed, or on the couch catching a quick nap, fantasizing about Ruthie and me walking hand in hand on some secluded Cape Cod beach and making love to the sound of waves crashing on the shore. There are no beaches and waves in Four Corners, and that's okay most of the time. However, a couple needs to build memories together of vacations that take the two of you out of your everyday life and give you a glimpse of the rest of the world," Ruth concluded as she wiped tears from her eyes again.

When Ruth arrived home from her trip to Watertown, Ruthie was busy making dinner, filling the kitchen with the aroma of a beef roast, freshly baked rolls, and freshly made applesauce. Ruthie had changed from her snappy-looking outfit from the morning, into blue jeans with a flannel shirt. AJ saw Ruth as she came in the kitchen door and ran toward Ruth with his usual happy bark. Ruthie turned around from the stove and smiled at Ruth. Ruth walked directly to Ruthie and put her arms around her, burying her head into Ruthie's back. They stood there for a minute, in silence, just holding one another.

"Nice to know I am missed, even when you are away for just a few hours," Ruthie said.

"Of course I miss you when we are apart, and it seems, lately, we have often been too far apart emotionally, even when we're in the same house," Ruth said. "I think we should talk about that after dinner tonight. But first, let me hear about your interview at the co-op," Ruth suggested.

"First, sit down for dinner before it's all burned," Ruthie directed, as she began dishing out the evening fare. After a bite or two, Ruthie began. "You may have to get dinner going on weekdays, starting December 1, because I will be getting home about 5:30 from my position as the co-operative's new bookkeeper," Ruthie proudly announced as a broad smile spread across her face.

"Congratulations, sweetheart!" Ruth shouted. AJ started to run under the table, upon hearing the shout, but Ruth picked him up before he could. "No, my dear little dog. This is a happy shout because your mommy had a great day," Ruth whispered in the little dog's ear. AJ started to wag his tail in obvious relief. "Dr. Spock says not to argue in front of the children because it traumatizes them. I guess that applies to dogs, too," Ruth said.

"One of the benefits will be that I can take AJ to work with me all day. Mr. Zimmerman said, 'If you can't take a dog to a Co-op Feed Store office, then where can they go?'

AJ loves to ride, so he'll just race to the car each day and go to work, too. I'll get a nice little bed for him for the office and take a few bones for chewing, and he should be just fine," Ruthie said.

"He'll always be fine as long as he has you. I have been," Ruth said. "Any other particulars about the job?"

"I get weekends off, so that will be nice for us. Government holidays are also vacation days. The first year, I get two weeks' paid vacation, as well as ten sick days, which may be accumulated from year to year. I will get three weeks' vacation after three years, and if I want to defer vacation weeks to another year, I can do that too. The best part is that I will be paid $650 a month, for a grand total of $7,800 per year. Wow, will we ever be able to save money then! That's as much as or more than you get paid, isn't it, even considering your merit raises the last two years?" Ruthie said.

"Yes, it is, Ruthie, but I didn't think we were in competition over money issues. I'll have to ask the school district for a raise to keep pace with you," Ruth curtly replied.

"Oh, I am so sorry, Ruth. I certainly did not mean to imply, in any way, that we compete with one another on that score. I didn't intend that at all. Why, I'd have to work several years before I caught up to repaying all that you've expended on us since my fall in the barn," Ruthie said, in a very caring voice.

"I'm sure you didn't mean to imply that, Ruthie," Ruth said. "Maybe I am a little upset that I won't have a 'wife' to come home to every night, with dinner all ready to eat. But I think this job is important for you and important for us. I want you to be happy, and I know you have not been so since you retired from farm work."

"It has been difficult for me, I admit. Hopping all over you, a couple weeks ago, when you got home so late from school, was a sign of my discontent, I think. I shouldn't have reacted that way, Ruth. I really apologize for that stupid fight we ended up having," Ruthie said. "Oh, and there is a little more to tell you about the job. I get to accrue a small pension, and I will be paying into social security again, which should help us have a comfortable retirement. Isn't that great?"

"Yes, my dear, it is great, and too bad we don't have some champagne to celebrate," Ruth said, as she thought about the fact that maybe this wasn't the best time to get into explanations for recent tardiness. How could she spoil this moment for Ruthie?

"Would some hard cider suffice for our celebration?" Ruthie asked, as she removed a sealed container from the refrigerator.

"Don't mind if I do," Ruth said. "This may lead to a wild evening. I didn't even realize you were keeping this stuff in the refrigerator. I like it when you surprise me with something out of the ordinary."

"I suppose now we could afford a glass of wine every night with dinner, if we weren't Methodists," Ruth said, just before taking a long sip of the cider and then smacking her lips in delight.

"What makes you think all Methodists are teetotalers? Over the years, I've smelled some liquor on the breaths of many farmers around here. They just avoid having it on their breath at church," Ruthie explained.

The two women drank all their cider and even had a second glass. Ruth thought this would not be the best night to have a discussion about her "conferences" with Paul at Clayton. Ruthie was so happy about her new job, and Ruth did not want to spoil their celebration. After a third and final glass of hard cider, Ruthie suggested they put AJ out for the night, turn off the lights, and go to bed.

Once they fell into bed, Ruthie pulled Ruth into her arms and asked, "Is this a night you are too exhausted from school to re-educate me about the way Smith College women make out? It's been awhile, and I might have forgotten my magical moves."

Ruth didn't hesitate. She began to kiss Ruthie passionately and massage Ruthie's whole body with her incredibly soft hands that Ruthie remembered noticing the first night they explored each other's bodies. It wasn't long before Ruthie began to feel things she had not felt in a long time, and soon exploded into pleasure, as a tear trickled down her cheek.

"I guess I can still give you tears of joy, my love?" Ruth inquired.

"You sure can, sweetheart," Ruthie replied. Without skipping a beat, Ruthie turned on her side, fondled Ruth's breasts, and slowly moved down to the place she knew gave Ruth fulfillment. She was so happy to hear Ruth encourage her to be forceful and move up and down Ruth's body until Ruth's whole body was exploding into pleasure, as she hugged Ruthie even tighter. Ruth lay in Ruthie's arms, enjoying her own body and wondering why it had been so many months since they last made love.

Ruthie turned her head so she could look directly into Ruth's face and said, "My God, you are beautiful. When we are in bed like this, holding each other, giving each other pleasure, it is as if we have melted right into one person. Do you feel that way too, sometimes?" Ruthie asked.

Ruth gave Ruthie another lingering kiss and said, "I get lost in your arms, Ruthie. You not only lift me up physically, but you lift me up emotionally, and I feel like we are the only people in the whole world who matter. My mind is freed from all cares and concerns, and it is only you who matters."

The feelings between Ruth and Ruthie were so intense and pleasant that night that they made love a second time, and then collapsed into their pillows. "What magical potion did you put in that cider?" Ruth chuckled. "There's a new song the kids are listening to these days, 'Love Potion Number Nine.' Did you sneak some of that into your cider?"

"No, I didn't need to do that. I have wanted you so badly

for so many weeks, but you always seemed too tired, and I also thought back to all the days I told you 'no' to lovemaking in my last couple years on the farm. I didn't push the issue, but I now understand how important it is for us to be intimate with one another, because it makes you fall back in love."

CHAPTER SEVEN

Ruth let only one week go by before she finally told the truth about her prior meetings with Paul. She could not remember another occasion in their fourteen-year relationship that she had been evasive, or had withheld any information from Ruthie. While their friendship with Billy and Cindy hadn't substantially changed, she knew, through their looks at her during this Sunday's church service, that they were disappointed at her hesitation to sit down and discuss her Clayton meetings with Paul. There had been much to celebrate with Ruthie's new job at the co-op, and that had been the sole focus of their conversations with Ruthie and Ruth at dinner the night before.

As Ruth played the last hymn of the morning, "Breathe on Me, Oh Breath of God," she resolved to tell Ruthie everything about Paul Slater. As she sang the lyrics of this old standard hymn, she asked God for courage to speak the truth, as well as courage to receive Ruthie's response, whatever it might be.

When they got home from church, Ruth encouraged Ruthie to relax in the living room while she prepared their dinner. Ruth wanted this time to go over, in her mind, just how she would explain to Ruthie that, while she had no reason to hide from Ruthie her time with Paul, she nevertheless had done just that. Any halfway intelligent human being would be suspicious of her explanation, and Ruthie was going to feel hurt.

After dinner was finished and the two companions lingered over their coffee, Ruth finally began. “Ruthie, I have a confession to make to you, which I’ve been withholding for a few weeks.”

Before she could start her next sentence, Ruthie chimed in laughing, “Let me guess, you took some extra money out of our coffee can to buy that new outfit you have? You must know I never count the money because it doesn’t matter to me how much is there. We both agreed we would put extra money from our pockets and purses in the can, from time to time, as our emergency money. If you took some for that outfit, I’d consider that an emergency. We can’t have the intellectual of Four Corners running about in rags, now, can we?” Ruthie said as she winked at Ruth.

Ruthie was making this so difficult for Ruth, because what Ruth was about to tell her would test the strength of their love. “Ruthie, please let me speak. This is serious stuff, really,” Ruth pleaded.

Ruthie stopped chuckling and was anxious to find out what could be so wrong about anything Ruth had done.

"I am sorry, sweetheart. I won't interrupt again. What is it you want to tell me?"

After one last silent request of God to help her, Ruth began again. "You know how late I have been, off and on, coming home from school since the fall term began? I was not completely honest with you about where I had been on those nights. Once a week, Paul Slater and I were driving in our separate cars to Clayton and meeting at Dave's Fish 'n' Chips." As Ruth thought through her next sentences, Ruthie remained quiet, but stared directly into the eyes of this woman she cherished and idolized. No, this couldn't be! She was speechless and could not speak if she had wanted.

"Oh my God, this is not going well! I can see by that unbelieving look in your eyes." She was sure she knew what Ruthie was thinking. "Ruthie, Paul and I are not having an affair. I know everyone in Four Corners would probably believe that was a good thing, but it wouldn't be a good thing for me. It all started when--"

Ruthie immediately interrupted Ruth, "What do you mean by it 'all' started—what is the 'all' that started! I am not an idiot. I've always seen how the men around here look at you and wish you were going home with them. I know you dated men at one time. I can't imagine you sleeping with Paul before breaking things off with me. You have too much integrity for that. But are you experimenting with dating men again by seeing him, and how many times have you met him in Clayton?" Ruthie demanded.

"Oh honey, I am not dating Paul either. The first week of school, he dropped by my office and asked me if I would be willing to go with him, for an hour or so, to Dave's in Clayton. I immediately put to rest any notion that this was a date and knew that you would have dinner waiting for me at home, so I didn't think it was a good idea for me to go to Clayton. He knew that day, when he walked into my office, that you and I are companions and he had no intention of disturbing our relationship in any way," Ruth tried to explain.

"So, what would you call these rendezvous hours with Paul? You're not a cocktail hour advocate normally. Is this some new Ruth I never knew existed?" Ruthie asked.

"Whether you want to believe me or not, this is the whole story. He told me that first night, he wanted to go to Dave's because he was in a 'very dark space,' and needed a confidante. He trusted me to be that person. He seemed very downcast. I think I have reason to accurately describe his depression, because I have worked with him for thirteen years now. And you need to think about that, Ruthie. If he wanted me as more than a friend, why would he wait thirteen years to take me out? I was twenty-nine when he met me, and now I am an old and gray forty-two," Ruth stated with great emphasis.

"Oh, come on now, Ruth, you are more attractive now than you were at twenty-nine, with that salt and pepper thick hair any aging woman would die to have. You have practically no wrinkles on your face, not even crow's feet. You must see that when you look in the mirror. Add in your incredible sense of style in clothing, and there is no other more attractive woman in the area, not even blonde-haired Cindy," Ruthie countered.

"You've always put me on a pedestal where I don't belong, Ruthie. That's part of our problem. I don't want, or deserve, to be on anyone's pedestal. If I am attractive, it is the good Lord who made me so. Is it so wrong I like nice clothes, perfume, and costume jewelry? Accepting what you say I am, should that preclude my being friends with a gay man?" Ruth said.

"A gay man!" Ruthie shouted. "Are you saying Paul is gay? For God's sake, if that is the case, why didn't you tell me weeks ago? I always wondered how he got into his late thirties without a wife," Ruthie said.

"I should have told you the very first night I was late that this was why I was late. However, this gets to our problem we need to resolve fourteen years into this marriage, if we are to remain happily together for the rest of our lives. You must know, after our wonderful night last week, that we connect physically in a way we could not do with anyone else. My heart is yours for as long as you want it. But please, don't imagine me on a pedestal, unable to have other friends and social contacts—just a statue, bereft of human emotion. Probably you and I work well as a couple because, on the level of values, including fidelity, we are just the same. However, our personalities are very different. I like having lots of friends. You will always be my best friend, but you can't be my only friend. Paul has become a good friend who has been working out, through talking to me, the predicament of being a gay man in a conservative, unforgiving place," Ruth concluded.

Ruthie sat back in her chair and asked Ruth if there was any coffee left in the canister. Ruth was relieved that Ruthie's voice had changed to a softer, kinder level, without an accusatory tone. She also knew her lover well enough to know that Ruthie was absorbing the comments she had made about needing other friends.

"Darling, we should never strain our relationship like this. I'll admit to being very jealous of you and your time. I need to work on that. I know I am somewhat of an introvert. Yet I also know I would not want to live without you, so if that means you need other friends in your life who will not lead you into their bedroom, I'll adapt. I don't want to be like that Mr. Stringwell who used to go to our church and got arrested for imprisoning his wife in their home, while telling us all that she couldn't leave home because she was dreadfully sick. Well, she was dreadfully sick—sick of him—and they were divorced as soon as she got out of that house," Ruthie said.

"There is no way you could become a Mr. Stringwell, Ruthie. If you mean what you say about me being so damn attractive to you still, you wouldn't leave the house long enough to tell anyone anything about me. Given your re-kindled libido—and thank the good Lord for that—you'd take me up to the bedroom and stay with me in bed until we died of heart attacks from too much exercise," Ruth said, as she winked at Ruthie.

"Well, my blood pressure has been great these days, and the doctor says I need to continue exercising for my heart's health. What do you imagine would happen if I tried to keep you here with me sounds pretty good to me. What a way to go! Can you imagine the headline in the *Watertown Daily Times*? 'Two Naked Middle-aged Women Found Dead in Bed in Four Corners'? People around here, except for Cindy, Billy, John, and Paul, would be terrified, especially, when the article went on to say 'The cause of death is undetermined, pending results from the coroner? While there appeared to be no forced entry into the home the two women had shared for some time, with no sign of blood or violence, their small dog was found cowering under the bed after the State Police broke down the front door.' Everyone would think there was a serial killer loose," Ruthie said, laughing until tears rolled down her cheeks.

Once their laughing had finally stopped, Ruth suggested they go into the living room. Ruthie was still too giddy to resist and followed her command, plopping down on the couch. Ruth made sure all their blinds were closed and then foraged through their record cabinet, pulled out a 45, and started up the phonograph, saying, "I am sure Paul has nothing on you in the dance department. After all, remember who taught you to dance!" Ruth pulled Ruthie up off the couch and "Be My Baby" by the Ronettes began to play.

"I didn't know you had this record!" Ruth said.

"The first moment I heard this song on the radio, on my way to work two years ago, I immediately thought of you. I had to buy it for us, only somehow, we never got around to playing it. Ruth whispered the lyrics in Ruthie's ear, as they found a way to waltz to the song. Ruth led the way through their dance moves at first, but then Ruthie took charge, pulled her still-gorgeous girl to her chest and sang sweetly along to the lyrics.

No passionate lovemaking was needed that night. Just falling asleep in each other's arms, some quiet whispers back and forth between the two women was enough. Together they had created a wonderful world in this place, this time, this love. Nothing else mattered.

CHAPTER EIGHT

March 1, 1968

It was Ruthie's 48th birthday, as well as the day before "niece" Ellen's 13th birthday, and there was much to celebrate. Once the whole Clayton misunderstanding was resolved by the end of October 1966, Ruth and Ruthie seemed closer than ever. Both were very busy with their jobs, with Ruthie noticeably happier having a job to go to each morning. It went without saying that all the co-op farmers were ecstatic with Ruthie's bookkeeping and all the special little greetings she sent to them each month with their checks. Ruthie not only included a handwritten note asking how the farmer's whole family was doing, but she took the initiative, after approval of the co-op board, to begin a monthly newsletter.

With her mechanical finesse, Ruthie had resurrected an old mimeograph machine, discarded by the church, and found appropriate parts to get it running like new. The newsletter included reports from the agricultural college at Cornell University, discussing yearly crop yields and suggesting better farming practices. The newsletter also contained long-term weather reports, a new recipe each month that required the use of dairy products, and an easy crossword puzzle drawn up each month by her friend John, who had a penchant for designing these puzzles. She also had a column at the end of each school term that read "Milk Makes You Brighter," and she would list all the farm children who had made the Honor Roll at school. Niece Ellen, was always on that list. Ruthie always asked Ruth to proofread the newsletter before she sent it out, and Ruth was happy to do so. Ruth rarely found any mistakes and would often think it was too bad Ruthie hadn't gone to Cornell to become a veterinarian, because she was whip-smart and a perfectionist.

Ruth had invited the family over for dinner to celebrate Ruthie and Ellen's birthdays. Ruthie was never one for big celebrations, but always welcomed the celebration of her birthday if they were also celebrating Ellen's birthday. This was the year Ellen became a teenager, and her parents were already worrying about hormonal outbursts and adolescent moodiness. Ruthie and Ellen had become very close, and Ruthie kept telling Billy and Cindy they had nothing to worry about because Ellen clearly had her head on straight and was incredibly mature for thirteen. Ruthie had been a math whiz in her high school days, so as Ellen moved into the fine points of algebra and geometry, Ruthie was always there to tutor her. All the other school subjects came naturally to Ellen, and between Ellen's mother and Aunt Ruth's recipes, they made sure she brought home A's in home economics, too, unlike her Aunt Ruthie.

The family circle had diminished, substantially, after the tragic car accident last year that ended the lives of Mr. and Mrs. Packer, the parents of Billy and John. During the winter of 1967, the Packers were returning from grocery shopping in Watertown when they were hit head-on by a drunken driver. Ruthie insisted on helping John and Billy with some farming chores the month following their parents' deaths, and Ruth baked, as well as cooked, a whole month's worth of meals for Cindy. It was a real emotional blow to the whole community, especially since the man who ran into their car was a former football star at the high school and a member of Four Corners Methodist Church. No one seemed to know the young man had a problem with alcohol.

It was a cold and snowy evening as the rest of the clan gathered at Ruth and Ruthie's for a delicious chicken and biscuits dinner, Ruthie's favorite. "I guess March is in like a lion, and hopefully leaving like a lamb," John said.

"According to my father, it was more brutal than this the night I was born," Ruthie mused. "It was so bad that night, Ellen, that Dr. Ralph had to deliver me right there at home," Ruthie explained.

"Was it like that for me when I was born, Mom?" Ellen asked Cindy.

"Oh, heavens no, sweetie. Your Aunt Ruthie was absolutely determined to see you were born in the hospital and had been wringing her hands, as well as walking the floors of her home, for a week, wondering if you, too, would be born on March 1. She listened to the weather reports on the radio every hour on the hour. Called your dad to see how I was doing and told him she insisted on driving us to the hospital, which she did very skillfully at 10 p.m., March 1, with a light snow falling that night. You were born one hour after we got to the hospital at 12:01 a.m., March 2, 1955, and your Aunt Ruthie remarked, 'Well, she tried for March 1, but everyone should have their own special day.'"

"Aunt Ruthie, we will always share our birthdays together, one way or another," Ellen said, giving Ruthie a peck on the cheek, with everyone smiling at the young girl's natural sweetness. Ruth looked over at Ruthie and smiled as she saw a tear rolling down Ruthie's cheek.

If ever Ruthie could have had a daughter, it was precious little Ellen. She was very much on the thin side like her mother, but wiry and athletic. She was left-handed like her Aunt Ruthie, who had practiced with Ellen to obtain fine penmanship even when her elementary teachers had given up trying. Ruthie had told her at the time that left-handed people were particularly talented and since she liked playing softball so much, she'd be an extraordinary first baseman, if she wanted. She was already 5'7" and would probably grow a couple more inches in height.

The hours Ruthie had spent throwing softballs back and forth to Ellen were incalculable. Billy would frequently watch this practice and often exclaim, "Look at the wing on that girl, Ruthie! I swear she could throw that ball all the way from outfield to home base without any trouble," to which Ruthie would always reply, "She inherited some strong arm muscles from her dad, for sure."

This year, for her 13th birthday, Ruth and Ruthie had splurged for a 10-speed bike. She more than deserved it, they told each other, for all the help she gave them around the house, weeding the garden, helping move furniture about when Ruth decided it was time to "shake things up a bit," and babysitting AJ if they were going to be away from home for more than eight hours on a weekend. They had put the bike in the garage, covered by a blanket, and waited until it was gift opening time to take her out to the garage, flip on the light, and uncover the shiny red bike with all its gears, a cushioned seat, and red streamers coming out of the handlebars. Their motive for splurging was also designed to get Ellen over to their home quicker from the Packer farm, and they were seriously worried about how rickety her old bike had become.

"I can't believe it," Ellen yelled when she saw the bike. "My very own 10-speed. Thank you, thank you, thank you," she gushed, as she turned around and gave both her aunts big hugs. Her brother stood aside, somewhat jealous, but he had to admit his aunts had never spared their pennies when it came to him, either, remembering the expensive telescope they had purchased for him just two Christmases ago. Just to make sure they remembered to continue to do so, Billy, Jr. spoke up, "Does this mean my rich aunts will be getting me a car in two years when I can drive?"

"For goodness sakes, Junior, how forward and rude of you," Cindy scolded.

Ruth and Ruthie laughed heartily, and then Ellen said, "All good things come to him who waits." With that comment, everyone laughed at Ellen's quick wit.

When they went back into the house, Cindy handed Ruthie a big envelope to open. "Well, what in the world is this?" Ruthie mused. She reached into the envelope and pulled out a receipt showing payment of a two-week cottage rental near Provincetown, Massachusetts. Also in the envelope was a map of Cape Cod, Polaroid pictures of the cottage that overlooked the ocean, a list of seafood restaurants on the waterfront, and $200. Ruthie's eyes filled with tears and she said, "This is just too much. I can't accept this," she protested, knowing what a tight budget Billy and family had to keep.

"You most certainly can," Cindy said authoritatively. "That wonderful woman standing right next to you said you needed to start seeing the world, and she is financially responsible for the rental. The money is from us, so you can see Ruth gets her fill of New England clam chowder and lobster. Billy even checked with the co-op to make sure you could get the time off in July, and when they heard it was a birthday present, the board was overjoyed to make that time available. So, no excuses now, you are going!"

Ruthie hugged Cindy and Billy, and then turned to Ruth with a smile, saying, "I guess I'll get to hear those waves crashing against the shore that you always talk about, after all."

"You most certainly will, Ruthie," Ruth said, with a wink and distinct twinkle in her eye. Only Cindy really knew what that wink meant, and she was happy for her two best friends.

CHAPTER NINE

Paul Slater announced early in the 1967 fall term that he had agreed to take a district superintendent job just outside Syracuse, beginning with the 1968-1969 school year. He had been at Four Corners for fifteen years, and it was time to move on. He had become comfortable in the small circle of gay men his partner had introduced him to, and he had certainly paid his dues, driving back and forth from Syracuse to Four Corners every weekend.

The new position for Paul came with a substantial pay raise, allowing him to buy a very nice home where he hoped his partner would join him. Even if that didn't happen, he knew he would feel so much freer in the city of 250,000. As the months ended on his Four Corners tenure, he wanted to do something very nice for his wonderful friend, Ruth. There was no doubt he would not have survived these last three years at Four Corners but for Ruth and Ruthie's friendship. Ruth had given him confidence that there was absolutely nothing wrong with him as a gay man, and when he went to Ruth and Ruthie's home once a month for dinner, he saw how much love they shared, and he wanted that for himself. Of course, most of the gossip around Four Corners was that Paul was probably getting close to asking the imaginary girlfriend in Syracuse, whom they had created for him, to marry him.

He would be presiding over his last Four Corners Alumni Banquet the first Saturday of June, and he thought it would be nice to start a Teacher of the Year award. He discussed the idea with the president of the student body and suggested the senior class could vote as to who would receive this award. He knew they would vote for Ruth because she was the star that lit up Four Corners School District, with every student she had ever taught raving about her brilliance, kindness, and belief in all her students, regardless of their academic abilities. Having overseen discipline since 1964 as vice principal, the students who got in trouble at the school had always believed that Vice Principal Packer disciplined them fairly.

He wanted the award to be a surprise as to the recipient until the banquet night. It would be easy to explain Ruthie's presence there, too, because the high school from which she graduated had been incorporated in the Four Corners School District, so she was an alumna. At each banquet, they had a graduate from each of the classes whose reunion years ended in a 5 or a 0. It was often the valedictorian of the class who made brief comments about what the school experience at Four Corners had meant in the life of that class, also noting members who had died since graduation. This was the 30th reunion of Ruthie's Class of 1938, and the only difficult part in the whole process of having Ruthie present to see her companion being awarded Teacher of the Year would be to get her to the occasion in the first place. She rarely went to the annual alumni banquet, even when she had been asked to represent her class. He knew he'd have to call in Billy Packer for this secrecy and collusion.

When Billy was asked to meet Paul Slater in Clayton at Dave's Fish 'n' Chips, he could not imagine what this could be about, except he was told on the phone it had to do with his cousin, Ruth. Once seated, with burgers ordered and coffee poured, Paul began.

"Billy, as you know I am leaving Four Corners School District on June 30, so this will be my last alumni banquet. Your cousin Ruth has been an extraordinary friend and colleague to me, and I can't imagine staying this long in Four Corners were it not for her good judgment, intelligence, and professionalism. She deserves to be acknowledged, in some way for all this, so I thought we should get the seniors to vote on the teacher they liked best during their time at Four Corners and give Teacher of the Year to that person. I asked them to secretly cast ballots as to whom they would want to receive this award. I knew they would pick Ruth, and when I counted the votes with the help of the school secretary, it was a landslide victory for her.

"I've asked you to join me here for a quick meal to figure out a way to get Ruthie to this banquet, so she can see

Ruth awarded this prize. I've been told Ruthie doesn't like large social affairs, and I've observed she usually doesn't go to the annual Alumni Banquet. I also know from my conversations with Ruth, in our early years as colleagues, that Ruthie and you have always been best friends, and this is your 30th high school reunion. Do you think you could possibly convince Ruthie to be your class speaker this year and attend?"

Billy was so glad to hear this news. He had always been so proud of Ruth and glad that she had found Ruthie as a life partner. Of course, Ruthie should be there. "Well this is all wonderful news about Ruth, and I will guilt Ruthie into going to our 30th reunion as only I can do sometimes. I assume Ruth knows nothing about this?" Billy inquired.

"No, she doesn't. I'd like it to be a surprise for everyone. Even the seniors will not know how the ballots were tabulated until that night. I'd appreciate it if you would keep this confidential. As for Ruthie, if you think you will need to tell her about the Teacher of the Year award to get her there, then I suppose that will be okay, because I think she has enough integrity to keep that secret," Paul said.

Billy assured Principal Slater that he would have Ruthie there one way or another and proceeded to tell him how fortunate Four Corners had been to have him in their midst all these years. "We will miss you, Paul, and I know my cousin is already anxious about your replacement. She keeps saying the school district will never have a quality man like you as principal, ever again."

"You know, don't you, Billy, that I tried to get the Board of Education to consider Ruth as my replacement, but they underlined the fact that every one of the applications involved men with advanced degrees in administration. I can tell you that means very little to me when it comes to feeding students' brains and souls. Ruth could do that like no one else could ever imagine. I tried to get Ruth to get her master's degree in education right after I asked her to be my vice principal. They have programs now where you can spend two summers on campus as well as complete a thesis at home and receive a master's degree. I think she might have gone for it, but then Ruthie's fall occurred, and the turmoil of all that set that possibility aside," Paul said, as he sadly shook his head.

"No, I never knew or even thought about that possibility for Ruth. It is a shame how the unexpected troubles of life seem to prevent a very capable person from becoming all they could be. I guess that's what happened here. Yet, if you asked my cousin if she had any regrets deferring her further education to take care of Ruthie, she would say 'No, this is what God needs me to do, and I will never regret having done so.'"

"Well, this is another reason I want Ruth to get this award. It is time we all recognized the sacrifices she has made for the school, the church, and for Ruthie. She does what she does because she is a woman of incredible integrity and humility, with never a thought for herself," Paul said.

Billy smiled broadly as he asked for the check, and said, "This burger is on me, Paul. Thank you so much for doing this for my cousin."

CHAPTER TEN

Billy had to guilt Ruthie into going to their 30th high school reunion, as well as being the speaker for the class of '38.

"Ruthie, you are so patriotic, especially since your brother Walter's death in Normandy. We've lost four male members of our class in World War II as well as the Korean War. The surviving class members know Walter was the first soldier Four Corners lost in World War II and would be expecting you to speak for their class, as you are recalling all these lost classmates. You owe this to Walter, Jr., if no one else," Billy pleaded. "I've been told if you are not the speaker for the class of 1938 this year, they will make me do it, and you know how I abhor public speaking!"

"Okay, Billy, okay. I will do my duty to the memory of my brother and our class of 1938. But you are going to sit right beside me, along with Cindy and Ruth. I know Ruth will go because she feels obligated, as vice principal, to go every year, and all in all, I think she enjoys it," Ruthie said.

Ruth was very surprised, but happy, to learn that Ruthie had been browbeaten into going to the alumni banquet by

Billy and that he had even convinced Ruthie to say a few words for the Class of 1938. Ruthie had attended this social affair only once since they had become companions, but Ruth attended every year since becoming a part of the Four Corners faculty in 1953. It was rare that the two of them went to anything with Billy and Cindy other than church. When the four of them got together privately for dinner and pinochle, sometime during the evening Ruthie would converse with Billy about the co-op and farming, while Cindy and Ruth talked about women at church who were having problems, or discuss the latest fashions and recipes.

Ruth even wondered if she was married to the right Ruthie when Ruthie indicated she would probably need a new outfit for the banquet, and since she was getting a new outfit, it was only fair that Ruth got a new one, too. With a successful trip to Watertown, both ladies had new suits with silk blouses. When they emerged from their home on the night of the banquet to carpool with Billy and Cindy, Billy whistled his approval of their outfits while Cindy just said, "Wow!"

All banquet attendees were treated to a delicious chicken dinner, complete with homemade pies prepared by the mothers of this year's Four Corners graduates. Once most of the nearly 150 people present had put down their forks after dessert, Paul Slater stood to start the program. A representative was present for every class starting with 1928 when Mrs. Hancock recalled how much smaller the school was in her time, forty years ago. After the Class of 1933 spokesman recalled how the Great Depression had made times very hard for the students, it was time for Ruthie's recollection. With a loud, clear voice she began.

"I am very honored to say a few words on behalf of the Class of 1938, and since most of you know me to be a woman of few words, that's what they will be." A few quiet chuckles could be heard about the room, with broad smiles appearing on the faces of Ruth, Billy, and Cindy. Ruthie continued: "We live in a time that seems fraught with chaos not only at home, but, once again, far away across the seas. We sometimes see our neighbors arguing with one another about how we should best resolve the war in Vietnam, treat civil disobedience at home, and enforce strict standards as to what an individual should be allowed to say, or how they should dress and behave in public. There has been even more discord over the Vietnam War since the death of our own Wade Kingsley, just two years ago. Some scholars say my generation had it very hard because we went to school during the Great Depression and then had to face World War II immediately. I want you to know that my brother, Walter Stein, Jr., along with four other members of our Class of 1938, believed the United States of America was the greatest country in the world because of the freedoms we enjoy every day. These men shed their blood in faraway lands, so we could have these debates with one another about what is or isn't a just war. Democracy is alive and well when reasonable men can differ. We should allow one another the freedom of differing opinions, while continuing to respect one another and care for one another. I believe, with all my heart, that this reverence for free thought, free speech, and freedom to act according to our conscience, was what the Creator has intended. Our forefathers believed this to be so, as well, and sanctified the concept by giving us the Constitution. Let us not tear the Constitution apart by hatred for our neighbors who see the world through different lenses. God bless you Class of 1968 as you go forth to honor this legacy."

As Ruthie sat down, everyone rose to their feet to give a rousing applause, much to Ruthie's surprise. As the clapping continued, Ruth sat back down, leaned over toward Ruthie and said, "Blessed are the peacemakers, for they shall be called the children of God." Billy made Ruthie stand up again and bow her head in thanks; then he gave his old girlfriend a big hug. He wanted everyone to know why this remarkable farm woman had been the object of his affection before marrying Cindy. Ruth knew how profound her partner could be, and what a shame Ruthie never got the college education she deserved. Whenever she would say that to Ruthie, her partner would always reply, "I might have never met you if I had gone to college, and then how happy would I have been without you?"

The class reunion speakers continued through the Class of 1963. The senior representing the Class of 1968 walked to the microphone with something in his hand and said, "I have the distinct honor of starting a new tradition for our alumni banquets, which will be to honor, each year, a teacher whom the senior class feels has helped them the most through their education here at Four Corners. The teacher will be selected by a secret ballot of the senior class members. It was also decided that the inaugural winner would have this award named after him or her forevermore. I actually do not know who this teacher will be, since Principal Slater and the school secretary counted the vote, and placed the results in this envelope," the senior explained, as he tore into the envelope. His face brightened as he read the slip of paper and announced "By unanimous vote of the senior class, the Teacher of The Year for 1968 is Ruth Packer, and this award shall forevermore be designated as the Ruth Packer Teacher of The Year Award, presented to our favorite teacher each year."

Ruth could not seem to move out of her seat. Billy and Ruthie had to get her moving toward the microphone and the sparkling trophy she was about to be awarded. She knew this award had been created just for her, and she knew Paul was, no doubt, responsible for moving the concept forward. She looked for a moment at Ruthie, with tears in her eyes, and then Billy came over to pull back her chair, guided her gently by the elbow the first few steps toward the head table. After she finally pulled herself together, Billy turned around and headed back toward Ruthie, smiling broadly.

Ruthie was smiling as well, and had a hunch Billy knew this was going to happen ahead of time. *That's why he bugged me so to be our class speaker this year*, Ruthie thought to herself.

Once she was at the microphone, the banquet room quieted, and Ruth began: "I suppose it is unimaginable for a middle-aged English teacher to say she is speechless, but that is exactly what I am. Like my dear friend Ruthie, I will be a woman of few words tonight. I need to thank the student body seniors who voted that I should be given this award. I need to thank my cousin, Billy Packer, Class of 1938, for convincing me to move to Four Corners in 1952, and to my friend, Ruthie Stein, who provided me with a way to remain here by taking me into her home when I had no place else to live. And, of course, I have endless gratitude to God, for working in mysterious ways, to provide me with the best teaching experience I could ever have. Finally, I must thank Principal Slater for offering me a position on this faculty in 1953 and being such a good friend all these years. I am going to miss you, Paul, more than you will ever know."

That was it. Ruth turned around to hug the student body president, and to give Paul a knowing hug and kiss as all present sat wondering how in the world the two of them never ended up marrying one another. They were so perfect for one another. Were they not crazy, avoiding a lifetime of companionship that marriage would have provided?

When she got back to her seat at the table, Billy and Cindy gave her big hugs; then she turned to Ruthie, who was still standing with all the others, clapping, and gave Ruthie that special hug no one else could see, but Ruthie would feel all the way to her heart.

CHAPTER ELEVEN

The trip to Cape Cod could not have been better. The July weather cooperated nicely as they took their time driving south and onto the Massachusetts turnpike. Ruth had gotten Ruthie to agree to visit Smith for a short stroll around the campus. Ruthie said that would be okay if she was shown where Ruth had her first kiss from the woman Henrietta. For some stupid reason, Ruthie thought about this Henrietta every now and then, wishing that she, herself, had been the only woman Ruth ever kissed. When Ruth led Ruthie off into the secret spot in the nearby woods, she showed her the big oak tree she remembered from that occasion.

Ruthie said, “Come here, gorgeous, and let me teach you what a real kiss is all about.” Ruth feigned being shy as Ruthie went up to her, cupped Ruth’s head in her hands, and tenderly kissed her lover of sixteen years. “Tell me that was far superior to that aggressive Henrietta,” Ruthie smiled.

“No question, my love,” Ruth answered as she snuggled into Ruthie’s shoulder. “Thinking back on that time, it was good you were not here, because if I had met you at Smith, we would have no doubt been thrown out for immoral behavior. They did that from time to time, you know," Ruth said.

"God had a plan for us, Ruth. I really believe that. We had to go through some misfortune before we met, and after we met, to understand what is truly important in life. There is only one journey that is worth the trip, and that is the journey into someone's heart who has been waiting for just you to continue the journey with them," Ruthie said.

Being middle-aged women wandering about the Smith College campus, Ruth and Ruthie felt free to take each other's arm as the old friends they were, walking with quiet conversation toward their car. Ruth had arranged for the two of them to spend one night in a charming bed and breakfast in Northampton.

It was partially overcast as Ruth and Ruthie drove toward Cape Cod the next morning, but it was very sunny inside their car. They both felt a freedom of spirit they had not experienced before as a couple. They were far away from anyone who knew them and felt free to hold hands in the front seat, except when an 18-wheeler was adjacent to Ruth's car. Then they assumed a trucker would be able to look down into the car, and they didn't want any trouble from anyone on this vacation. They had discussed what public displays of affection they would allow themselves and had both agreed the only place they should feel free to be loving in public would be the Provincetown lesbian bar they had been told about by Paul.

The cottage that had been rented was near Eastham, adjacent to the Cape Cod Seaside National Park. They would be able to walk for miles along the beach or use the beach chairs and giant beach umbrella they had purchased in Watertown while they dug into all the paperbacks they had also brought along. When they arrived at the cottage, they were not disappointed. It was a spacious two-bedroom cottage with a front porch, supplied with two rockers and a porch swing facing the ocean. The kitchen was fully equipped and large enough for both to cook together, although Ruth said she'd be the cook, if Ruthie gathered wood for the living room fireplace which would be used when nights turned cold.

On the way to Eastham, the couple had stopped by a roadside fruit and vegetable stand, buying enough produce for at least a week. As they drove through the town, they spied a grocery where they would return the next day for some staples. They had packed some coffee, and Ruth had secretly baked and securely wrapped some raisin scones, Ruthie's favorite. Ruthie could arise tomorrow to the smell of freshly brewed coffee. But for tonight, they would relax and dine at Whale of a Menu diner, advertising fresh seafood and casual dining. Ruthie had eaten little seafood in her life, and Ruth was looking forward to introducing her to fresh fare.

Once they arrived at the restaurant, a handsome young man came over and asked, "May I help you fine ladies?" Ruth took over and told the young man they had driven a long distance that day, were hungry, and would like a nice view of the ocean. Ruth slipped him five dollars and they were promptly escorted to the best view in the restaurant, which also happened to be a big comfortable booth. They settled in as the young man asked if either would like a cocktail, which they politely declined in favor of some iced tea.

Ruthie deferred to Ruth to order for both. "Let me see what you should try," Ruth thought out loud. "I think you should have the seafood platter, which has haddock, fried shrimp, and clams, served with French fries and coleslaw, which I know you like. I am going to order the sole with red potatoes and asparagus. We can top it off with a piece of their homemade raspberry pie," Ruth said, as she put down the menu, letting the young man know they were ready to order.

While the women waited for their meals, they drank some iced tea and stared out a large window facing the ocean. As the sun began to set, rays of light danced over the waves, and they found no need to talk as they stared at scenery they had never shared before. Ruthie finally broke the silence. "God made a beautiful world, didn't He?"

"He sure did, and one beautiful part of it is sitting right across from me in this booth," Ruth said, as she looked directly into Ruthie's eyes and smiled.

"Since when did you become a brownnose?" Ruthie replied with a laugh.

"I'm not brownnosing," Ruth replied in a very serious tone. "The only real fault I've ever found in you, after sixteen years together, is that you don't see your own beauty. You were created to be strong and so very kind. You are a good woman, Ruthie, and I'm the luckiest woman in the world to be here with you," Ruth said.

"I guess there will be no 'I'm just too tired tonight' excuses allowed when we get back to that cottage," Ruthie quietly commented. The meals arrived, and Ruthie's fisherman's platter was huge. She tried the fried shrimp and clams first, raving about how delicious they were.

"Well, eat all you want, because it says 'all you can eat' right on the menu," Ruth said.

Ruthie had seriously cut back her food portions after her farming days, but her eyes were too big for her stomach, and she ordered some more shrimp and clams. Finally, after an hour had elapsed, they agreed they were stuffed and would take the pie to go. Ruth insisted on paying the tab and left a generous tip. The young waiter was very pleased and said to the ladies, as they headed out the door that he had learned something tonight.

Ruth had to ask, "And just what valuable life lesson did we impart to you, my good man?"

"I've always been told by the older waiters that women aren't the best tippers, and when two or more of them dine together, they take lots of time going over the bill to figure out, to the penny, how much they each owe, and they leave exactly 10%. That wasn't the case at all with you two fine ladies. You already had it figured out who was going to pay, and you never scoured over the bill for mistakes," he added.

"Not all women are alike, young man, and my dear old friend of sixteen years was enjoying her long overdue birthday meal. Ruthie and I go back and forth, treating one another, and we don't keep track of how much one pays over the other. It all works out in the end when you share, doesn't it, Ruthie?" Ruthie wanted to say something witty about being called her "old friend," but she'd wait until they were at the cottage to do so.

The drive back through a brightly moonlit night was almost magical. Ruthie drove to the cottage thinking about being in bed with Ruth, with their cabin windows wide open and the cool ocean breeze wafting in. As she thought about the passionate lovemaking to come, she suddenly felt like she was on fire with itches. "Oh my God, Ruth, I can't stand this," she screamed as the car swerved with her body as she tried to rub her back and shoulders on the back of the seat.

"What in the world is going on, Ruthie?" Ruth shouted. "You're going to get us killed with the way you are driving. Pull over, pull over! I'll drive us."

Ruthie did as she was told, exchanging places with Ruth in the car while scratching every piece of her skin she could reach. "They must have had little bugs in that restaurant that bit me everywhere," Ruthie screamed.

"Well, we're just one block from the cottage, and I'll take a look at your skin the minute we're in the cabin," Ruth said.

Once they were out of the car, Ruthie ran to the cabin door and flipped on the kitchen lights, so she could see her way to the bedroom. As she ran into the bedroom, she was shedding her clothes from her body as quickly as she could. Thank, God, they had not made up their bed before leaving for dinner because Ruthie flopped down on the sheets of the bed seeking relief from whatever had bitten her. Ruth had retrieved a flashlight and ran over to the bed to examine Ruth's back. She saw numerous hives all over Ruthie and then tried very hard not to laugh.

Ruthie looked at Ruth and groused, "What can possibly be funny about this? I'm in agony here and you think it's funny? Damnit, what's wrong, Ruth?" Ruthie demanded.

"Before tonight, Ruthie, had you ever tasted shrimp or clams?" Ruth asked.

"No, but they were delicious. Why is that important?" Ruthie asked.

"Because my dear land-lover, I think you are allergic to shellfish. I saw these same hives on a classmate at Smith who was allergic to lobster. I know you must be in agony. I am going to get a warm washcloth and wipe your back, arms and legs. I brought some calamine lotion with us just in case we ran into poison ivy and I will put some on each hive. That should help quite a bit," Ruth reassured Ruthie.

"So much for your plan to have me try new things! What's next? Taking me out on a sailboat when I don't know how to swim?" Ruthie said, just as Ruth came back with the calamine lotion.

"You never know; I might insist on taking you out in a sailboat. You don't know how to swim, but I do, and I would just love saving you," Ruth said, chuckling. "You see in the water, especially sea water, you'd be very buoyant, and my strength would be greater than yours. For the first time in our lives, I could just drag you all over the place like shark bait."

"Well, I'll make certain you don't have to save me, then. And to think I had wonderful plans for you tonight in this bed. Forget that, my dear. You'll be lucky to even get a kiss out of me. This is your doing, the way you kept saying 'Eat all the shrimp and clams you want, Ruthie. It says on the menu all you can eat.'"

With that comment, they both burst into laughter and kept laughing until tears were rolling down their faces, and Ruth grabbed her side as if she might burst apart. "I did say that, didn't I?" Ruth said, as she tried to catch her breath. "I guess I'll have to take my punishment and lie here all night, starved for affection and feeling sorry for you. That should make you feel better."

Ruth began to methodically daub each hive with some

calamine lotion, and with each application, Ruthie felt some relief. "How long will these things last, Dr. Packer?" Ruthie inquired.

"Hopefully, they will be gone by tomorrow, and this lotion will relieve the itching enough for you to get a good night's rest. We'll keep it a quiet day tomorrow, and I'll go to the grocery for some chicken or beef to cook for dinner. I have a nice surprise for you tomorrow morning," Ruth said.

Ruthie groaned. "I can't wait for your next surprise!"

CHAPTER TWELVE

The next morning when Ruth awoke, she realized she had instinctively snuggled onto Ruthie's shoulder during the night. Ruthie was sleeping soundly, and Ruth took a minute to think how she might exit the bed without waking her hive-ridden lover. The bedsprings did make a lot of noise, she had noted last evening, as they tried to get Ruthie comfortable for the night. Somehow, she was able to gracefully get out of bed as Ruthie rolled over on her side and continued her sleep.

Ruth put on some Cape Cod-appropriate clothes and started the coffee percolating. Fortunately, they were just down the street from a newsstand, so she raced out the door to get a *Boston Globe* and a local newspaper. When she got back, the coffee was done and giving off that amazing aroma which, for her, made the morning glorious. She retrieved the scones and cut up some cantaloupe, setting the formica dinette table with luncheon plates and coffee cups. She went into the bedroom and leaned over, giving Ruthie a soft kiss on her forehead.

"Wake up, beautiful lady," Ruth said. "Your surprise awaits at the breakfast table."

Ruthie opened her eyes and smiled. "What makes you think I want to get out of bed for one of your surprises? Answer me this—does your surprise involve me eating something I've never eaten before?" Ruthie asked.

"No, sweetheart, it doesn't. No more food surprises on this trip, I promise. Let me look at your back and see how those hives are healing." Ruth could see the hives had substantially diminished in size, and some had even vanished. "How well you recover from ailments, Ruthie. You have the most incredible immune system," Ruth said.

"Good thing when I'm traveling about with one of the ladies from *Arsenic and Old Lace*," Ruthie joked. Ruth retrieved some clothes for Ruthie and headed to the kitchen. Ruthie smelled the wonderful aroma of coffee and told Ruth she'd be right there. When she was dressed, she walked into the kitchen and saw a steaming hot cup of coffee, fresh melon, and her beloved scones. Ruth was already preoccupied reading the *Boston Globe*.

"Wow. What a treat! I think I'll just throw caution to the wind and eat these inviting scones with that wonderful coffee, and some fresh melon, to boot." Ruthie gave Ruth a kiss before she sat down.

"This is what you would call a 'continental breakfast,' Ruth said as she smiled at Ruthie and then returned her attention to reading the *Globe*.

"I don't care what it's called; it's delicious," Ruthie mumbled as she consumed her scone and took a large gulp of coffee.

"It's nice and sunny today. I thought we might stay close to the cottage, sitting in the rockers on that nice front porch overlooking the ocean. When we're done this morning with breakfast, I'll run to the grocery and get some luncheon meat, chicken to fry in the skillet for dinner, and any other staples we'll be needing this week," Ruth said, as she continued to read the paper.

"Whatever you think is best, sweetheart. Reading, rocking, looking out over the ocean, maybe listening to a few songs on our transistor radio would be great. What did you bring along for us to read, Professor Packer?"

"Quite a variety, including that controversial *Valley of the Dolls*,

The Fixer by Malamud for me, *The Confessions of Nat Turner* for you, since you love history, and *Rosemary's Baby* to scare ourselves to death some night reading in bed," Ruth replied.

"Sounds like a good collection, except for that last one. I can think of better things to do in bed than scaring ourselves to death. Haven't we already had our first night in bed ruined? Do we need more?" Ruthie kidded Ruth.

"Alright, alright, alright. Mea culpa again for last night," Ruth replied. With that having been said, Ruth got up from her chair and poured Ruthie some more coffee. Then she went into the bedroom and retrieved *The Confessions of Nat Turner*, helped Ruthie get comfortable on the front porch, and headed to the grocery.

After putting the groceries away, Ruth walked to the front porch and saw that Ruthie was engrossed in the Nat Turner book. "I see you like your history book," Ruth said as she picked up *Valley of the Dolls* and took her place on the porch.

"My goodness, Ruth. Had you ever read these accounts of the brutality done to the slaves? I knew they were not treated well at many plantations, but it was just disgusting how they were brutalized," Ruthie said. "They certainly gave us a watered-down account of what really went on, in the American history textbooks at school," Ruthie frowned as she returned to her book.

"Yes, it is disgusting how blacks were treated and how they continue to be treated. If only more people were to read that book you're holding as well as *Uncle Tom's Cabin*, maybe this country could make more progress toward civil rights. No wonder they are rioting in the streets, especially with King shot down in April. We stay very isolated from those events, as we exist in all-white Four Corners," Ruth agreed.

They continued to read all day as they occasionally looked up from their books and watched the seagulls sailing and swooping toward the beach below. They ate a late lunch on the porch, and as some clouds rolled in, they agreed to take a nap before fixing a late dinner. Ruthie's hives were nearly gone, and she opened her arms wide for Ruth as they snuggled into the squeaky old bed. "How did we ever get so lucky to find each other?" Ruthie said.

"We are not lucky, honey; we are blessed. God wanted us to go through this life together, and that's just what we're doing, the best way we can, with a whole world of misunderstanding about just who we are outside the door every day, everywhere," Ruth said.

After four days of walking the beach and eating Ruth's great cooking, the couple decided to drive to Provincetown, have dinner, and go to the lesbian bar Paul Slater had recommended. After eating the "sunset special" at The Oceanside Café, the ladies began their adventure at the Lavender Lounge. As they entered the smoke-filled bar, they saw several women dancing to "I Can't Get No Satisfaction." It seemed like a mostly young crowd, but there were a few middle-aged women and they felt the eyes of these women latch on to both of them. "Well, this is interesting," Ruthie said, as she searched for a booth or table where they could sit down. She whispered to Ruth, "What's that woman over there all about? She has the shortest hair I've ever seen on a woman and a t-shirt with one of the sleeves rolled up around a pack of cigarettes. She has men's shoes on and a cigarette behind one ear!" Ruthie shouted into Ruth's ear to compete with loud rock music.

"Shush, she'll hear you. When we find a place to sit down, I'll try to explain," Ruth said. When they finally got seated, Ruth quietly explained about the butch-femme subculture of lesbianism. Ruth knew about this from her own conversations with Paul, who had run into some of these women during his past visits to gay bars in New York City.

Ruthie was aghast. "To each her own, I guess, but what I like about women has nothing to do with that. I like softness and curves and femininity."

"I'm sure that's what she likes about women, too, by the looks of her beautiful girlfriend she's now kissing," Ruth chuckled.

"Oh, my God, are you saying that's how you see me!" Ruthie asked.

Ruth couldn't keep herself from laughing. "No, honey, I don't see you just like that, but I do like those farm muscles you have, and I like it when you literally sweep me off my feet and kiss me sometimes," Ruth answered with a smile. She urged Ruthie to go get them a couple of drinks from the bar, and she would hold down their booth.

"What can I get you, my princess?" Ruthie teased. "Everyone seems to be drinking beer right out of the bottle. I'm not a beer fan. Wine's more my style, as you know. But what do you want?"

'I'm going to throw caution to the wind and have a Tom Collins, and later a tomboy on the side," Ruth smiled. "No problem with that second round," Ruthie winked back.

The bar was quite busy, and it took a few minutes to get the bartender's attention. Finally, as Ruthie turned around to carefully carry the drinks through the crowd, she saw one of the butch women sitting across from Ruth, chatting away. She had a feeling she was going to spend the evening fending off single women in the bar. When she got to the booth, she said, in a most authoritative voice, "Honey, is this woman bothering you?"

The woman stood up and faced Ruthie directly in the eye. "You sayin' this is your girlfriend?" Ruth watched the interaction with fascination. She knew Ruthie was a peace-maker, and not a fighter, and from this woman's body posture, Ruth could tell she was challenging Ruthie to a fight.

Ruthie quietly set the drinks down and told the woman, "Why don't you ask this gorgeous woman, yourself, if she's my girlfriend? I can predict her response after sixteen years of living together," Ruthie said with a very calm voice.

The woman obviously didn't know quite what to say. Finally, she offered her hand to Ruthie for a handshake. "If you two have been an item for sixteen years, that's all I need to know," she said as Ruthie shook the woman's hand, squeezing it with every muscle she had in her arm and hand. She watched the woman retreat to the bar shaking her fingers. Then the woman started talking to a group of her friends, pointing over toward Ruth and Ruthie's table.

Instead of sitting across from Ruth, Ruthie slid in next to Ruth in the booth, gave her a big kiss, and handed Ruth her Tom Collins. Ruth put her head on Ruthie's shoulder and whispered into Ruthie's ear, "You're pretty sure of yourself, lady, when it comes to me, don't you think?"

"I suppose I am, my love. You know I adore you, that I've never wanted any other as my best friend, as well as my lover. And I think I may not be gorgeous like you, but I have my good points," Ruthie said.

"That you do, Ruthie, starting with those beautiful kind eyes and smile." Ruth gently kissed Ruthie and took her hand. Just then, Frankie Valli's "Can't Take My Eyes off of You" came on the sound system, and Ruthie asked Ruth if she wanted to dance. Pleasantly surprised by Ruthie's overtures, Ruth nodded, and together they moved to the dance floor and enjoyed being able to slow dance with one another, in public, to a song filled with so much truth for both. They never seemed to get tired of staring at one another, even after sixteen years of spending every day together.

After a couple more dances, the two lovers decided it was time to go home to the cottage. They drove quietly along the highway adjacent to the ocean, watching the moon and stars, as well as the waves ebbing and flowing on the beach. They held hands and enjoyed the ocean air entering their open car windows. Finally, Ruth broke the silence. "Our first time dancing in public together was nice, wasn't it?"

"I have to admit that it was. You taught me well about dancing in the privacy of our living room, so I wasn't too self-conscious about taking the most beautiful woman in that bar into my arms, letting everyone know she was mine," Ruthie said.

"That I am, your lady forever. I'm not sure you're right about me being the most beautiful woman in that bar. There were several cute girls half my age in that place. Some had been staring at you off and on during the evening, Ruthie."

"Well, I never saw that happen, but if you say so, I'll take your word for it," Ruthie replied. "There was not one girl in that bar who comes close to 'turning me on' as they say these days, as you do," Ruthie said, as she raised Ruth's left hand to her lips and gave her hand kisses. They drove on in silence, once again listening to the waves lap on the shore.

Arriving at the cottage just before midnight, the couple made short work of locking up for the night and going to the bedroom. They undressed each other without saying a word and slipped under the sheets, taking turns slowly moving their hands to the places they knew would send the other into ecstasy and release. It was through these acts of giving their bodies over to the other that they felt the assurance of being right where God intended them to be. It was an experience of spirituality as their souls united in this physical expression of love.

When they were done making love, Ruth assumed her usual place on Ruthie's shoulder. "I think this evening was just about perfect—don't you, sweetie?" Ruth whispered.

"It was all wonderful, except for that brief moment I had to contemplate taking down that fireplug of a woman who wanted to fight me over you," Ruthie laughed. "I kind of wondered if that was what you wanted me to do, and why you didn't immediately intercede verbally."

"Well, first I kept quiet because I knew it was highly

unlikely you would fight her. Second, I knew you were way too bright as well as too much of a lady to resort to fist fights in a bar when you could out- debate her any day of the week. I mean, what would a good Methodist think about such an altercation! Third, maybe I was a bit excited by watching you fight for me, my Sappho in Shining Armor. Fourth, I knew when push came to shove, you'd flip her on the floor without hurting her, so fast she wouldn't know what happened," Ruth laughed.

"You know how I knew that?" Ruth continued. "Remember that young Black Angus bull my dear cousin Billy had given you to raise for meat, and how it got loose, running all over the barn floor terrorizing the cows? It was just before your mother died, and we were still trying to tiptoe around each other about being in love with one another. I was still trying to figure out every facet of your personality. Well, when that little bull got loose, you were yelling and hollering at the baby bull so loudly I heard you all the way in the house. I came running to the barn and saw you chasing that wayward Angus all around the barn. I begged you to let me call Billy and ask for his help, and just as I was suggesting this, you grabbed that rascal and flipped him right onto the concrete, holding him down until I got some rope to tie him up. That act was most impressive. I thought for a moment that I certainly didn't want to get on your bad side! So, in the bar tonight, I just knew that lady would hit the deck if she tried to seriously fight you," Ruth said.

"I never knew that sort of thing impressed you," Ruthie said, as she yawned loudly. "I'll have to ask Billy to let me do more steer wrestling for your enjoyment. I do remember calling him up after that incident, informing him I wouldn't be raising his beef cattle any more. I'm not so sure, at forty-eight, I could do that little stunt again, except when it comes to you; I most certainly would put my body in front of yours to protect you from any danger, even if it meant being gored by a bull. But a butch woman? No problem; she'd be on the floor."

With that, they both laughed and fell off to sleep. Every year after 1968, Ruth and Ruthie rented the Eastham cottage for two weeks. Each summer they expanded their lesbian social circle on the Cape, becoming particularly close to Ruby and Eileen, a Jewish couple from New York City, who owned a cottage in Eastham. Ruby was a staff medical doctor at Lennox Hill Hospital in Manhattan, and Eileen was an editor at Random House. They had met one another at Radcliffe in the late 1950s and had been together since. They were impressed with how much Ruth and Ruthie still loved one another, as they struggled with the boredom of their own relationship. They invited Ruth and Ruthie to visit their apartment in Manhattan, but so far, the Four Corners couple hadn't found the vacation time to make the trip.

Ruth and Ruthie explored the possibility of buying their rental as a second home, utilizing the cottage three weeks each year, and renting it out the other summer and fall weeks. In 1971, they made an offer to the owner that was satisfactory and accepted. Because of their frugality in Four Corners, they were able to pay cash. They hoped that when they retired, they could live in Florida for the winters and spend the summers on Cape Cod.

CHAPTER THIRTEEN

May 1972

While Billy, Jr. prepared for his high school graduation as valedictorian and enrollment at Cornell University School of Agriculture, Ellen was doing very well academically, too, yet finding more time than Billy, Jr., to help on their dairy farm. Billy had really come to appreciate his daughter's work ethic and her physical strength. She reminded him so much of Ruthie that he sometimes absent-mindedly called Ellen "Ruthie." He would then apologize for this slip of the tongue, to which Ellen once replied with a smile, "If I remind you of Aunt Ruthie, that's a good thing, because Mom told me you once thought of her as your girlfriend and wanted to marry her. I can see why you liked her, Dad, because while she isn't as pretty as Mom, she sure is kind and thoughtful as well as super bright. I would not have passed algebra or geometry if it were not for Aunt Ruthie."

"Nor would I have passed those courses when I was in school, but for Aunt Ruthie," her father said.

Other than girls' basketball and softball, Ellen showed more interest in the farm animals than other extracurricular activities. She was selective when it came to friends but did have a best friend named Brenda, whom the two aunts had seen with Ellen on several occasions, as she stopped by their home for a weekly visit. Ellen had grown to almost six feet and was slim like her dad, with very dark brown hair and blue eyes. Her friend, Brenda, was very cute at just 5 feet 2 inches, with blonde hair, blue eyes, and a smile that lit up the whole room.

One day, as the two girls left Ruth and Ruthie's home after dinner, they watched Ellen open the car door for Brenda and they could hear them both laughing. Ruth turned to Ruthie and remarked, "Do they remind you of anyone?"

"You mean us?" Ruthie asked. "Well, I think that's quite possible. Billy tells me that Ellen seems to have no interest in boys, even though several boys have asked her out. She likes her farm chores and has told him she wants to be a veterinarian. She believes if she works hard enough at her academics, she can get scholarships. She appears to use studying as the reason she has no time for dating. I also watched Ellen look at Brenda when Brenda was talking to us. Ellen looked smitten," Ruthie concluded.

"Do you think the feelings are reciprocal?" Ruth asked.

"Well, I sure hope so, because it would be easy to see how a cutie like Brenda could break someone's heart," Ruthie replied.

"I agree. I love Ellen so much; I'd hate to see her have to go through all that misery of a love lost," Ruth said.

"They are still so young. Remember, we were thirty-three and twenty-nine when we went to bed for the first time, and that was several months after we were living together in the same house, but sleeping in separate bedrooms," Ruthie observed.

"Yes, but these are different times, and since Stonewall three years ago, there has been so much public discussion about whether homosexuals should be treated so badly. Most of us are still 'in the closet,' as they say, but I'm not sure Ellen's generation is going to feel it is so terrible to be gay," Ruth said.

"I hope you are right about us being recognized as not so abnormal," Ruthie sighed. "But I think it will take a lot longer than you think to be viewed in the same way as straight couples are viewed. We will certainly never be allowed to get married. It will take a lot of strength to be an openly lesbian couple, unafraid to let others know they love one another. If Ellen and Brenda are a couple, I am sure we will be the first to know," Ruthie said as she shut the back door.

The next month, Billy, Jr. graduated from Four Corners School District and comported himself well as he gave a very good valedictory address. His aunts were very proud of him and gave him a generous monetary gift to use at Cornell. It was the Packer family plan to see Billy, Jr. was well educated and up to date on the latest farm practices, and if he decided he wanted to farm, as well, his father had his eye on a third farm he might purchase.

Life seemed good for Ruth and Ruthie. The principal who had replaced Paul, Winston Buckholtz, seemed somewhat spineless, which had resulted in more public relations work with the parents, as well as disciplinary work for Ruth. However, he left her alone and never criticized her work. There was nothing to criticize. Ruth had become so good at getting the graduates placed in various colleges and universities that the Board of Education agreed with Principal Buckholtz that Ruth be relieved of any teaching duties, allowing her to concentrate on guidance counseling instead. She also got another pay raise that she immediately banked for their retirement.

Meanwhile, Ruthie still enjoyed her work at the co-op and she, too, had received a substantial pay increase. She had to admit that apart from the drive to the co-op in blinding blizzards at times during winters, she felt good about herself. She loved asking AJ if he was ready for work every day, which sent his tail wagging furiously. All the fellows at the co-op really liked her and AJ, and every Friday she would bring them home-baked cookies that either she or Ruth made each week. The boys laughed about how all their wives were jealous of the quality of the cookies they raved about every Friday when they got home. There was also the factor of Ruthie's daily coffee-brewing perfection that she gladly performed for her male colleagues. She was cagey enough to stroke their egos by seeking all their opinions as to what truck she should buy to help her plow through the snowy roads. All the men at the co-op knew about Ruthie's terrible tumble on her farm that had ended her farming career and left her with arthritis and a slight limp. The guys were very protective of Ruthie and would not let her carry or lift anything.

The only thing that had gone awry in their community, as far as Ruth and Ruthie were concerned, was the replacement of their beloved Pastor Hutchinson with an older pastor who loved to preach hellfire and brimstone, with frequent altar calls so people could be "born again" into the grace of God. One Sunday, Reverend Dooley got shouting so loudly about going to hell unless you gave your life to God that a little seven-year-old girl in the congregation, Charlotte Grayson, started crying hysterically. Her mother was beside herself with embarrassment and tried to comfort her, but to no avail. Ruth could see the fright in the little girl's eyes and very quietly tiptoed over to Charlotte and asked her mother if she could take Charlotte into fellowship hall for a cookie and some milk. Mom nodded affirmatively, and Ruth whispered in Charlotte's ear, "I bet a cookie and some milk might help, don't you think?" Charlotte stopped crying and took Ruth's hand as they quietly exited the sanctuary.

Rev. Dooley tried to make light of it by chuckling, "At least I know one congregant understands what the fear of

God is all about." No one laughed. Ruthie was furious about Rev. Dooley's ranting and raving about hell and was so glad Ruth had taken Charlotte away from the reverend's tirade. Everyone in the church looked up to Ruth, and by volunteering to calm Charlotte down, hopefully, other worshippers would regard the reverend's preaching as over the top.

Once Charlotte sat at a table and was chewing on one of Ruth's famous oatmeal cookies, as well as drinking some milk, Ruth began to talk softly. "Did the pastor scare you, Charlotte?" Charlotte nodded. "Well, honey, there is no reason for you to fear hell, because you're not going there, sweetie. In fact, Jesus loved children more than adults, and Jesus never wanted anything bad to happen to children. In fact, He told some adults one day that unless they became more like little children, they could not be His followers," Ruth explained.

Charlotte had listened very intently. In a very hushed voice, she asked, "Why is the minister so worried about people going to hell? He's going to heaven, isn't he, and he'll just have more room in heaven if lots of others are going to hell?"

Ruth couldn't restrain herself from laughing, as much as she tried. When she finally stopped laughing, realizing that the people in the sanctuary could probably hear her loud laughs, she quietly said to Charlotte, "You are so smart, honey. When you graduate from high school, I have just the college for you."

Charlotte, a little bewildered, but much more relaxed, smiled at Ruth and simply replied, "Okay."

Ruth could not get back into the sanctuary to play the last hymn but didn't worry. "Amazing Grace" could easily be sung a cappella, and she knew Rev. Dooley would be glad to lead, given that the song mentioned wretchedness.

Ruth waited in the fellowship room for Charlotte's mother. When Mrs. Grayson got to fellowship hall, she thanked Ruth profusely for coming to her rescue and added, "You know, Miss Packer, I want my children to always behave in church, but Rev. Dooley was way too loud this morning, and I am not surprised Charlotte got scared. I'm sure he means well, but someone should tell him to calm down a bit, don't you think?"

"Yes, someone should, and I think the sooner the better," Ruth said in a very exasperated voice.

Once they were in the car on the way home, Ruth and Ruthie compared notes on the church service. When Ruth told Ruthie about Charlotte's thoughts that the reverend should want people to go to hell so there would be more room in heaven for himself, Ruthie laughed and laughed. "I wish someone would tell Dooley to go to hell!"

"Well, if he keeps frightening children, it may be me who tells him," Ruth said. "Did you ever hear of Jonathan Edwards and the great evangelical awakening in 18th century America? I probably wouldn't have known about him if I hadn't gone to Smith. His ministry began right there in the

Congregational Church of Northampton about 125 years before Smith College opened. Well, this Edwards used to preach hellfire and brimstone so vividly that people would faint from fear. He described to the congregants how they would be dangled over the pits of hell if they did not give their souls to Jesus," Ruth explained. "Some say he was the forefather of the evangelical movement."

"Rev. Dooley must be the great-great-great grandson of Jonathan Edwards on his mother's side," Ruthie suggested sarcastically.

"Cindy is on the Pastor-Parish Relations Committee. We should convey to her that some parishioners are concerned about Rev. Dooley's too aggressive preaching style. Maybe the committee can calm him down," Ruthie said.

It was the third week in June when Rev. Dooley came back from the Annual Conference of the United Methodist Church. He gave a report about what had been discussed and decided by the elders and representatives of the church.

"Perhaps, some of you have heard about a homosexual rights movement in America. We, United Methodists, are against this abhorrent behavior and have made our *Book of Discipline* reflect that stance by inserting new amendments stating that 'homosexuality is incompatible with Christian teaching' and no 'self-avowed homosexual' will be ordained by our denomination. Let's praise God that

His Spirit has moved within our church to place us on the right side of history on this issue. There are so many evil forces within our society, but homosexuality is the worst of all sins. It requires all God-fearing Christians to be soldiers for Christ and stand up against this depravity."

As Rev. Dooley preached on about the wages of sin, Ruthie sat up a little straighter and glared at the pastor. Ruth didn't dare to look at her partner but could well imagine Ruthie fuming inside. Ruth had begun to dread her piano-playing duties, now that she had to listen to Rev. Dooley's uneducated theological pronouncements. This sealed it for her. She would wait a week or two and then step down as the congregational pianist. It wouldn't be hard for the congregation to understand that after twenty years, she was tired. It was certainly going to be an interesting ride home.

As Ruth played the last hymn, Ruthie gave Billy and Cindy a big hug, quietly exited the church, and waited in the car for Ruth. Billy and Cindy knew she was getting out of the church ahead of the others, because she was madder than a hatter about what had just been said. Ruthie had been glaring at the pastor, as well as clenching her right fist so tightly that she had drained it of any blood. Ruthie wanted no part of shaking Rev. Dooley's hand at the church door.

Both women wanted to get far away from the church property before they began their discussion of Rev. Dooley's verbal attack on the homosexual community. Ruthie began the discussion. "It is bad enough that we have to listen to that fool every week, but now we are told we are not Christian in the eyes of our denomination. What's the point of wasting our time at that church when we're going to hell!"

"I'm right there with you, my dear," Ruth said. "Rev. Dooley is an ignorant, judgmental man who doesn't deserve our support, and as far as the whole denomination becoming homophobic, I don't know where that leaves us."

"I know where it leaves us—it leaves us right outside that church," Ruthie sputtered. "We were comfortable there as long as we hid our love for one another, and, unfortunately, we still have to do that because of our jobs, particularly yours. When the subject of homosexuality never came up in the church, we looked the other way and just kept living our lives with no guilt, because we knew we had been brought together by God. We must find a way to quietly exit that church. If we don't go to church next week, it might be too obvious that we were offended by new church pronouncements about the sinfulness of the gay life, and people would put one and one together, as far as we're concerned."

"Well, I'm not sure all of them would, because most people just can't imagine two women together in any other form than housemates or spinsters. However, I can think of much better ways to spend our Sunday mornings than in this drafty old church. Just imagine us sleeping in and getting up at our leisure, lingering over coffee and a great breakfast. As far as spirituality is concerned, we experience that every time we just sit quietly together, hold hands, and talk about the people we truly care about in this community. We can even get *The Upper Room* mailed to us and go through a whole week's meditations discussing them together," Ruth said.

Ruth continued her thinking out loud. "In one month, we go to Cape Cod for three weeks, as we now do every year. Just before we leave, I'll tell that pulpit dolt I want to give up the pianist position after twenty years. That is not a strange request. No one will ever question why I'm stepping down. Also, you've been telling me that you've developed so much arthritis in your right hip, you sometimes feel a bit unstable. When we get back from the Cape, you'll be using a beautiful cane we'll find for you on the Cape. Those stairs into the church are killers. I'll tell them you need some time to recuperate before you can navigate them, and we'll just never go back. You can take that cane to work with you, and those nice boys at the co-op will treat you even more like a princess."

"That sounds like a possibility, and let me say we have done so much for that church over the last two decades, I feel no remorse about leaving. Sure, we might miss seeing some of our church friends, but we get lots of contact with the community through our jobs, and I very much like the idea of having Sunday mornings free for ourselves. Who knows what we might decide to do on a lazy Sunday morning?" Ruthie said as she reached for Ruth's hand to hold.

The church participation ended just as they had planned it. Many parishioners telephoned Ruth and Ruthie to tell them they didn't know what they would do without them. One lady from the Women's Fellowship said the whole group was beside themselves with the loss of two long-standing members. Ruth told Ruthie that it was a comment on how much they missed their cookies, dues, and work at bake sales and church dinners, as well as rummage sales. Ruth added that if they knew they were lesbians, the ladies of the church would be appalled and want nothing to do with them.

"Why hide in a volunteer organization that doesn't want us to live our truth? Jesus doesn't want us to be hypocrites," Ruth said.

CHAPTER FOURTEEN

May 1973

Ellen appeared at their door about 7 p.m. the first Saturday in May with huge tears rolling down her cheeks. She was just six weeks from her own high school graduation, and with her second cousin's help, she had been accepted on a full scholarship to Smith. Since she was a second cousin to a successful alumna, she was considered a legacy at Smith. What a celebration they had for her the night of her 18th birthday, when she had just heard about her acceptance! The world seemed to be Ellen's oyster. What had driven her to tears? Ruthie wondered, as she let Ellen in the back door of the house.

Before she could even close the door, Ruthie found Ellen sobbing in her arms. Her sobs were so loud that Ruth came quickly from the living room to see what was going on. Ruthie was just tall enough, and strong enough, to hold Ellen upright as her body-wracking sobs continued. Ruthie wondered if Ellen's parents were hurt or dead. "My dear, dear, niece, what in the world is wrong?" Ruthie said, as she hugged Ellen with all her might.

Ruth walked quickly to their sides and softly patted Ellen on the back, stating, "Whatever it is, you've come to the right place, because we'll move the world to fix it."

Ellen stopped the sobs and asked for some Kleenex. After she blew her nose, with a stuttering voice Ellen said, "I have no doubt I've come to the right place, but you can never fix what has just happened to me." The tears started again, and her aunts gently guided her to the big comfy chair in the living room, with Ruth turning off the television.

"What is it we can't fix, my dear?" Ruth said.

"I'm a little embarrassed to talk about it," Ellen said, as she blew her nose again and stared at her feet.

"You should know by now, sweetie, there is nothing you could say to us that we wouldn't want to hear, and we will love you always, no matter the problem," Ruth replied. "Just tell us."

Ellen took a deep breath and began. "You know my friend, Brenda? She wasn't just my friend; we loved each other, or at least I thought we did until tonight." Ruth and Ruthie gave each other a knowing smile while Ellen used the Kleenex again. "Apparently, Brenda's mother found a love letter I had written her that she stuck between her mattress and bedspring. Her mom was changing the linen on Brenda's bed when she found the letter. She confronted Brenda with the note when Brenda got home from school yesterday. I'm not exactly sure what her mother said to her, but Brenda called me this morning and asked if I could talk freely on the phone. I thought that was kind of a strange question, but I told her no one was around me in the house just then. It sounded like she was crying, and of course, that alarmed me. I asked her if she wanted me to come over to her house, and what was making her upset."

Ellen continued talking, taking deep breaths every now and then. "Brenda told me about the letter her mother had found, and her mother was very angry. She told her to have no further contact with me whatsoever. If she found out we were ever together alone outside school, she would call Principal Buckholtz, as well as Smith College, and tell them that Ellen Packer was a lesbian who was pestering her daughter. Brenda told me that if she agreed to stay away from me and have nothing to do with me ever again, her mother wouldn't say anything. Otherwise, as she threatened, 'That Packer girl won't be delivering any valedictory address, nor will she be going off to Smith.'" Ellen ended up where she had begun, a young lady sobbing her eyes out.

Ruth and Ruthie looked at one another and both understood the importance of this moment. It was a coming-of-age moment, as well as a horrible situation for their lovely, kind, thoughtful Ellen. Both women knew they needed to comfort and give advice to this woman who had experienced heartbreak for the first time in her life. Ruthie nodded toward Ruth, urging her to start.

"It is just horrible what Brenda's mom did to you and Brenda, Ellen; there is no getting around that. You no doubt feel as if your life is over and nothing can be fixed, but your other aunt and I will help you through this as best we can. To be honest with you, both Ruthie and I thought you and Brenda might be true girlfriends by seeing how the two of you stared at each other and seemed so affectionate toward one another, but we would never allow ourselves to assume anything. I am glad you came to us. Surely this demonstrates that you know Ruthie and I are more than just friends?"

"Billy, Jr. and I talked about the two of you from time to time, but our parents never told us the two of you were an item or anything. But the older I got, and the feelings I started having myself—especially toward Brenda—left no doubt in my mind that you two were more than friends. It is my assumption Mom and Dad know this, too, but were very protective of both of you and never told us anything other than you were both good, talented women who loved living together. Since you are really my second cousin, Aunt Ruth, I thought, my goodness, maybe there is a genetic connection between us that made us gay?" Ellen stared right into Ruth's eyes, looking for an answer.

"Could be, my dear second cousin. I'm not sure psychologists have figured out why we prefer women to men as our partners. For me and your Aunt Ruthie as well, it is easy to answer, because we truly believe God made us this way. And, whether people understand this as part of creation or not, there is evidence all about us that we are a natural part of creation. You can ask your Aunt Ruthie more questions about that. She's the one who put that concept in my head twenty years ago, when we first became lovers," Ruth said, with a smile.

At this point, Ruthie couldn't restrain herself from jumping into the conversation. "Oh, my precious Ellen. You are going through something that, somehow, God spared me from experiencing—heartbreak. How blessed I have been to have your cousin as my partner for twenty years and the first and only lover in my life. But I do know what it is like to look at a woman, like my Ruth, and have nothing but respect and love for her. The thought of us ever being apart is devastating. I had to grow up in our relationship to realize she was a separate human being, who had to have a life outside of just our life together. I wanted her around me all the time. So, this loss for you must be crushing, and I so wish I could spare you this heartache. Brenda is a beautiful young lady, and it seemed to me that she cared a great deal for you, but you must be practical about your future and hers," Ruthie advised.

"You need to stay strong when you feel like you are going to fall apart, and you will be able to do that because you have Ruth as your middle name, and Ellen Ruth Packer can get through anything, even something as horrible as this," Ruthie said.

"Do your parents know about your relationship with Brenda and what has just happened?" Ruth asked.

"No, I never talked to them about Brenda, other than our being in sports together and how smart she was. I just didn't have the courage," Ellen said.

"Actually, that is probably for the best," Ruth sighed. "It is one thing to have a cousin who is a lesbian and quite another to have a daughter who is. Your parents are very good people, and they will come to accept your sexual preference in time, but now is not the time to push that issue with them. We will see that they come to accept you, as you move through your college years. For now, say nothing and try to hide your sorrow as best you can. Come over here every night if you need to, and study your heart out so you can get that Regents Honor Diploma and maintain your valedictorian position in your class. Don't you worry about Brenda's mother. If she tries to get to Principal Buckholtz, he'll refer her right to me anyway, and I know just what to say to her without stirring up the controversy any more.

"As for Brenda's mother calling your parents, I sure can handle that," Ruthie said. "I would tell your father that Brenda's mother is a very vicious woman, and no doubt jealous of Ellen's accomplishments. I would go on to say that the two of you have been over here many times and we never saw anything untoward happening, which we haven't. If they ask you about a relationship with Brenda, you just tell them that Brenda's mother is spiteful, that you can't believe she has threatened Brenda with such a revelation if she remained your friend, and you have resolved to stay away from Brenda."

"Aunt Ruthie, I am not sure I can stay away from her. I love her so," Ellen began to cry again.

Ruth jumped in the conversation again. "We wish we didn't have to advise you to stay away from Brenda. You are both eighteen now, and theoretically, you could defy Brenda's mom and continue your relationship. But honey, it is way too much to risk to give away a bright, bright future for you, and hopefully for Brenda, too. When you go on to college you can write each other all the love letters you want. Until then, you need to stay away from Brenda. If you are worried about her taking your cold shoulder the wrong way, I can, as her guidance counselor and your cousin, call her into my school office and let her know I know what has happened. I will advise her that you want her to know you'll be in touch when the two of you are in college, if she wants to still see you. But for the sake of you both, she must stop seeing you right now," Ruth said. "May I ask you a very personal question, Ellen, about the degree of your sexual involvement with Brenda?"

"We have 'made out' many times, but we were actually saving anything more involved until the last week before we went to college, planning a short trip to Lake George to sort of consummate our relationship. We planned to say vows to one another on the waterfront, when no one else was around and make it seem like our wedding," Ellen said tearfully.

"That sounds very reasonable, yet exciting. Maybe you can do that on an autumn weekend in New England, when the foliage is so beautiful. If I recall correctly, Brenda is going to the State University at Albany in the fall. Wouldn't be too hard for you to get together then, if that is what you still want," Ruth said.

"Why wouldn't I want to do that? I'd like to do that now, but I am not an idiot, Aunt Ruth. I can see how unaccepted lesbian relationships are in our society and that you must be careful. For the life of me, I don't know why Brenda put that letter in that location in her bedroom, especially if she wasn't going to be changing her own bed," Ellen said with a measure of disgust.

Ruthie had been thinking that to herself as well. It could have been an intentional decision on Brenda's part to have her mother find this letter from Ellen as a way of ending their relationship. But for now, she only wanted Ellen to have some peace in her heart, if any was to be found, so she spoke up. "As they have always said on the farm, 'You can't cry over spilled milk,' and maybe Brenda just suddenly stuffed the letter between the mattress and box springs when someone in her house was approaching her room and then forgot she had put it there. It seems like a long time until you are off to college, but it's just a matter of weeks. In the meantime, as your Aunt Ruth has suggested, study hard, and come on over here anytime you want to commiserate about your broken heart. We do understand what it means to hold another woman in your arms, whom you love so much."

Ellen had stopped crying, completely, and went over to the couch, sitting between her two aunts. "I am so glad you are my aunts and that you understand. You have done so much for me already—tutoring me through math classes, Aunt Ruthie, and getting me into Smith, Aunt Ruth. And now, knowing for sure that two women I admire and love so much are just like me does help a lot," Ellen said, as she put her arms around both and gave them a squeeze. This gesture sent tears down both Ruth and Ruthie's cheeks.

Finally, Ruthie pulled herself together and asked Ellen, "Why don't you stay over here tonight with us? Just call your folks and let them know where you are and that we are going to have a late-night TV fest. We'll make some popcorn, drink some soda, and eat cookies while watching an old movie, or we can just talk. Whatever you want to do."

It was well after midnight when Ruth and Ruthie got to bed, after making sure Ellen was comfortable on their sofa bed. The couple had chatted a very long time with their niece as she asked them a million questions about what it was like "hiding in the closet." She did not go into any specific sexual questions, except to ask her two aunts if they still were close "that way" after twenty years together. They explained to Ellen that all couples, gay and straight, don't feel the need for nightly passion, and as they moved into their fifties, hormonal changes could make the sexuality between a couple a bit different. They told her, however, that they felt as much passion for one another as ever, and on their annual trips to Cape Cod they felt more relaxed to physically express that passion.

Ellen told them she had always enjoyed being around them because there was such a sense of kindness and peace between her two aunts, which made their home a refuge from the rest of the world. She told them her parents got along well, but she didn't see the same emotional closeness between them as she sensed between her aunts. Ruth replied that she was sure her cousin, Billy, was as much in love with her mother, Cindy, as ever, and that she should consider herself lucky to have them as her parents. Ruth went on to say that having dated men in high school, college, and Cooperstown, she learned that men looked at life and sexuality much differently than women.

"Boy, do they ever," Ellen said, as she rolled her eyes. "You know that Rudy Contino who is in my class, Aunt Ruth? Well, he asked me out a couple times. First time out was okay. We went to a movie and held hands during the movie, with him putting his arm around me in the movie theater and kissing me a couple times. I felt nothing when he did that, just nothing. However, I accepted this was just normal dating stuff, so I didn't protest.

"The next time we went out, he drove to the river where there is a lookout for lovers. I had a sense of dread I couldn't shake. Before I had a chance to say anything to him, he grabbed me and reached under my bra, fondling my breasts. As I heard him unzipping his pants as he moved on top of me, I kneed him as I pushed his head into the car console and said, 'What in the world do you think you are doing? I don't want this to go any further. As soon as I had my boobs back in my bra, I stepped out of the car, slamming the door,'" Ellen related forcefully.

"Good for you, honey," Ruth said. "Let me tell you that a true gentleman would have never done anything like that. I know we are in the middle of a sexual revolution, but I hold by the old standards of how things should go, even in straight dating. Everybody is in such a race to get physical in the dating process; it hardly gives either party a chance to know if this other person is even close to being the type of person you would want to continue dating, let alone, perhaps, take the relationship any further. You find out so much about one another just by being around each other and talking. I'll give you an example. The second-to-last man I dated in Cooperstown was very handsome, well educated, a brave Korean War veteran. My mother thought he was wonderful, so to please her, I didn't turn down a date. He took me out to dinner one night after we had been dating three months, revealing that while he was divorced from his first wife, they did have a little four-year-old girl named Judy. He said, and I'll never forget his exact words, 'I didn't really care for Judy when she was first born, but now I think maybe I should develop a relationship with her as she grows cuter and more verbal.'"

Ruth continued, "I sat there aghast, thinking to myself, what kind of a father does not love his little baby girl! By a baby's very nature, aren't they cute? He had informed me about the divorce shortly after we started dating, but never told me about his daughter until that night. I also admitted to myself I was not ready to be a stepmother to a child who barely knew her own father. That was it. I broke off our relationship the next time he called me, much to my mother's dismay."

Ellen seemed more at peace after this conversation with her two aunts and yawned widely. "I think you need some sleep, my dear," Ruth suggested. "Let's get this sofa bed all set up for you, and then we are off to bed, too." Ruthie pulled out the sofa bed as Ruth retrieved the bed linen and found an old nightgown Ellen had left at their home a few months back. They reminded her of the guest toothbrushes in the medicine cabinet and then went off to bed.

As they lay in bed thinking about their conversation with Ellen, Ruth asked, "Do you think Ellen will be able to stay away from Brenda long enough to get through her graduation and on to Smith with no trouble from Brenda's mother?"

"I certainly hope so. I am glad you felt bold enough to pry into their sexual relationship. We can still remember, after two decades, how much more powerful the connection becomes once you've moved past kissing and hugging. I know we are really from a different time, but I suppose orgasms haven't changed much since our first days together as lovers," Ruthie replied with a laugh.

"No, my dear, I am sure you are right about that," said Ruth, as she put her head on Ruthie's shoulder after giving Ruthie a good night kiss on the cheek.

CHAPTER FIFTEEN

March 1, 1975

It was Ruthie's 55th birthday, and Ruth invited Cindy and Billy to go with them to a new steak house in Watertown to celebrate the occasion. Before they left their house to pick up their best friends, Ruth told Ruthie she had a gift for her. She took a velvet ring box out of her pocket and handed it to Ruthie. Ruthie took the box and opened it to find a huge aquamarine ring with little diamonds all around the giant stone.

"This must have cost you a fortune!" Ruthie gasped. "You shouldn't have gone to this expense. It is just gorgeous, almost too fine for an old farm girl like me."

"No, my dear; you may be 'an old farm girl' as you say, but that is why I love you. You are the salt of the earth that hasn't lost her saltiness. You are the soil to my heart that has allowed me to grow and bloom with more love than I ever believed I could feel. No piece of jewelry can repay you for all that, but maybe, when you look at this ring you will remember how much I love you," Ruth said, as she watched Ruthie place the ring on her left ring finger.

"You sure you want to put that ring on your left finger? That's where one usually wears a wedding ring," Ruth said.

"Well, aren't we married, Ruth? It's been twenty-three years we've shared our home and our hearts. If people look at me strangely because of this ring on my left hand, let them surmise and think what they want. I'm fifty-five now, and they can believe whatever they want. If they ask me where I got it, I will tell them you gave it to me. It's as simple as that," Ruthie said, as she held her hand out and stared at the beautiful new ring.

"Well, aren't we getting brave," Ruth laughed. "I suppose it will be another item of interest for the Four Corners gossip machine. I agree; so be it," and with that, she took Ruthie's head in her hands and gave her a kiss. "You should look inside the ring too, Ruthie." Ruthie pulled the ring off her finger, and after retrieving her reading glasses, she read "R&R" with an infinity sign after the lettering. Ruthie's eyes were watering, and she gave Ruth one of her hugs. Both women stood embracing one another until Ruth reminded Ruthie they'd better be going, or they would be late picking up Billy and Cindy.

Their evening at the new steak house was wonderful. Unlike the day Ruthie was born, March decided to come in like a lamb, so the roadways were dry, coming from and going to the restaurant. They even decided to share a bottle of wine, which was just enough for one full glass each. It was not likely they would run into any Methodists from Four Corners, and if they did, Ruth said she'd tell anyone that it was she who tempted them with this drink by buying dinner, since it was Ruthie's 55th. She was already seen as a backslider since she and Ruthie no longer went to church.

"So, now they will know for sure I am going to hell," Ruth laughed.

Ruthie didn't have to bring up the subject of her beautiful new aquamarine ring, because Cindy noticed it right away. "Oh, my goodness, what a beautiful birthstone," Cindy said, as Ruthie then took off the ring and handed it to her. "It looks like there is something engraved inside. May I look?" Cindy asked.

"Please do," Ruthie said. After reading the engraving, Cindy handed it to Billy, and replied, "Truer words were never engraved. You two probably have the best 'marriage' in Four Corners, and we've had the honor to watch it grow and deepen," Cindy said.

"Ruthie and I have said to one another many times that our relationship flourished because the two of you emotionally supported us throughout these twenty-three years. Few couples like us have remarkable straight friends like you two," Ruth said. Just then, the waiter came by and handed the bill to Ruth, which she quickly paid with a generous tip, as well. Billy and Cindy objected to Ruth paying the full fare, but she ended the conversation by saying, "I am so blessed to have each one of you in my life; this bill is just my way of saying thanks."

Once they got home, they put AJ outside for a few minutes, as they both stood and looked at the star-strewn sky that seemed more glorious than one could find in other places they had visited. Ruthie could see Ruth's teeth were chattering, and so she stood behind Ruth and wrapped her arms around her to protect her from the cold north wind. "That feels so good, sweetheart," Ruth said, as she continued looking at the cloudless night sky. "You make me feel like we are in our thirties again," Ruth said.

"For tonight, let's pretend we are," Ruthie suggested. With that comment, Ruthie called to AJ, and their faithful little boy followed them into the house. Once in bed, Ruth asked, "You want your last birthday gift, my dear?" With Ruthie's smile and nod of the head, Ruth reached over to Ruthie, and slowly, but surely, made Ruthie feel like she was thirty-three again. It had been a few weeks since they last made love, but it was "all" right there again: the passion, the spiritual connection, the release from all worries. When Ruthie gently embraced and massaged Ruth's right breast, she was startled to feel a rather large lump. She said nothing until they were both laying in bed, holding hands.

"Ruth, have you noticed you have a lump in your right breast?" Ruthie asked.

"Oh, Ruthie, don't worry about that! I felt that about six weeks ago when I was in the shower. My mother had what you would call polycystic breasts, where lumps would form and the doctor would remove them, but they were always benign," Ruth said.

"But don't you think, in an abundance of caution, you should have it checked out right away?" Ruthie pleaded.

"I was planning to call the doctor at the end of this school term. I never smoked or took birth control pills—both things they have found that can contribute to breast cancer—so given my mother's condition, it is unlikely this lump means anything. If it will make you feel better, I'll call Monday and see if I can get in during Easter vacation, but as I said, it really is nothing to be terribly concerned about," Ruth said.

"Yes, it would relieve my mind to make certain it is nothing, and I will ask you when you get home from school Monday if you made an appointment," Ruthie said, as she gave Ruth one last good night kiss.

Ruth lived up to her word and scheduled an appointment with an ob-gyn doctor. The receptionist said the doctor would want a mammogram completed before he saw her, so Ruth scheduled that as well. On the day of her doctor's appointment, she was told that a surgical biopsy should be done, given the family history of polycystic breasts. Again, Ruth agreed, just to make Ruthie relax about this annoyance. The doctor's office scheduled the biopsy two weeks later.

It was another two weeks after the biopsy when the receptionist from Dr. Randolph's office called Ruth at school one morning, asking her to come in the next day to see the doctor in the afternoon. "Is that absolutely necessary?" Ruth inquired. "Can't I just get the results over the phone?" The nurse indicated the doctor did not discuss private health concerns on the telephone.

Ruth did not call Ruthie at the co-op to tell her she was headed into Watertown after school. There was no point in having Ruthie miss work and getting her all riled up. Ruth was smart enough to know the results of the biopsy were probably not good. When she got to the doctor's office, the receptionist took her to the doctor's office and not to an examination room. Dr. Randolph smiled politely and asked Ruth to have a seat.

"Good afternoon, Miss Packer," the doctor began. "The pathologist's report has come in finally, and I am sorry to say it is not a good one. The tissue removed was cancerous and is what we call a large grade 3 tumor. What this means is you need to have surgery to remove your right breast, at a minimum, and if we find cancer has indeed spread to the lymph nodes under your arm, they will be removed as well. Blood tests and x-rays will be taken to see if the cancer has spread to other organs, which is what we call metastatic breast cancer. There is no cure for metastatic breast cancer. We need to stay positive and hope the cancer is confined to the breast and lymph nodes. If that is the case, the cancer is treatable with radiation and chemotherapy. Do you have any questions?"

Ruth pulled herself together enough, emotionally, to ask, "When would I be having surgery?"

"I would like to do it as soon as possible, and I have a surgical opening for a week from today. We don't want the tumor to stay in there any longer than necessary. Can you arrange your schedule to have the surgery on that date?" the doctor inquired.

"I can do that," Ruth replied in a shaky voice. She felt tears surfacing and wanted to get out of the doctor's office as soon as possible. The doctor told his receptionist to put Ruth on the surgery schedule and to let Ruth know about when and where to report on the day of surgery.

As Ruth drove toward Four Corners, she burst into tears and had to pull over to the side of the road for a moment. After wiping her tears and blowing her nose, Ruth prayed out loud, "God, I admit I am scared. I can't be stronger any longer. I'm very angry with you right now. I wanted to grow old with Ruthie. We had it all planned out after we retired. Why now? Please calm my mind and my soul. Give me courage to get through this."

Ruth got back on the road and continued driving toward their home. It was officially "their home," because right after Ruthie's 55th birthday celebration, Ruthie had returned from work one night and handed her an envelope. When she opened it, she saw that Ruthie had put her name on the deed to their home as a "joint tenant." That was rarely done, in these parts at least. If women housemates owned a home together, they usually took the deed as "tenants in common," which meant half of the house would go to the deceased tenant's relatives. Ruthie pointed out to Ruth, "My only relatives left are a few rather greedy cousins who never had much to do with me, so why shouldn't the love of my life get the house?" If word got out they were joint tenants, everyone would know Ruthie and Ruth were more than just friends. "But who cares what they think?" she had said.

Ruthie probably had the state troopers out looking for her right now, because she hadn't phoned home to tell Ruthie she'd be late. When she pulled into the driveway, true to form, Ruthie raced toward her car. Ruthie yanked open the door and said, "Are you okay? I've been worried sick." Their eyes met, and Ruth started crying again. Ruthie asked no more questions and gently guided Ruth out of her car into the house.

"What's happened, honey? I've never seen you like this before. Cry all you need to cry. I've got you," Ruthie said, as she tightly held Ruth in her arms for a long time. Ruthie took Ruth's coat and had her sit at the table. Ruthie sat down right next to Ruth and said, "What's this all about? Did anyone physically hurt you? If they did, I'll kill them!"

Ruth composed herself, took a deep breath, looked at Ruthie and said, "I wish it were that simple, my Sappho In Shining Armor, but I have an enemy you can't fight off for me, Ruthie. I have breast cancer and I am headed for a radical mastectomy a week from today."

Ruthie slumped in her chair and wanted to cry herself, but she owed this remarkable angel who had come into her life every fiber of courage she had. “You must have gone to see the doctor after school? Is that right? Why didn't you call me to go with you, honey? What did he say exactly?”

“The pathologist's report came back indicating I have a large grade 3 cancerous tumor. My right breast must be removed and perhaps the lymph nodes as well. The doctor said, during this surgery, they'd be able to see if the cancer has spread beyond the lymph nodes. If it hasn't spread further, I can be treated with radiation and chemotherapy, or perhaps, a combination of both. If it has spread, that is what they call ‘metastatic breast cancer’ and there is no cure,” Ruth said. “I am not unduly afraid to die, Ruthie. It's just the disfigurement of my body that bothers me, and wondering if it would really be worth the bother to undergo further treatment if the cancer has gone further into my body.”

“First, why are you talking death?” Ruthie said. “The surgery may well remove all the cancer cells. And who in the world cares about losing a breast? It doesn't matter to me one whit.”

“Well, I care. I've always wanted to be beautiful in your eyes. Going to bed with me now is going to be a nightmare, and I don't want you to see me all mutilated,” Ruth said, with tears brimming in her eyes.

“Now, stop that talk, Ruth. We all grow old and become

less physically attractive on the outside, even without cancer. We get wrinkles, age spots, cataracts, arthritic everything, as we march on to the end of our worldly lives. You didn't love me less when I got this big scar from my fall in the barn, did you? Nor did you love me less when I could not make love to you for weeks after that fall. So, just tell me how you think our love will change or disappear? I am every bit as much in love with that soul of yours, your brain, your sense of humor, as I am that right breast, for God's sake," Ruthie said.

Ruth leaned into Ruthie's chest, as Ruthie gently stroked Ruth's beautiful hair, which had not thinned with time. Ruth added, "If I am really truthful about how I feel, I feel cheated. Remember that Robert Browning poem we used to read to one another from time to time— 'Come grow old with me, the best is yet to be'? I thought often about that phrase these last few years after we bought the house on the Cape, talked about retirement, and maybe wintering in Florida. Now, we may never get to do that, Ruthie."

"Well, we don't know if all those plans are dashed, do we? We can talk about this more after you've eaten your dinner warming on the stove. You need to eat to keep up your strength and keep that immune system fighting those cancer cells." Ruthie dished up their dinner, sat down at the table, and took Ruth's hand. "Lord, we need your peace and spirit in our hearts tonight. May this food strengthen my beloved Ruth, and may she be cured of this cancer, so we can be together for many more years. Amen."

Ruth squeezed Ruthie's hand and then began eating a bite or two of dinner. While she tried to eat, Ruthie reminded her that she would be with her throughout the whole hospital ordeal and come in every day to see her after the surgery. Ruthie went on to describe how she would bring her back to their home, to heal and to rest, with AJ right by her side every minute. "This is a nightmare that will soon be over, sweetheart," Ruthie assured her love.

Ruthie got a warm-up for Ruth's tea and told her to keep eating while she ran a hot bath for Ruth that would relax her, and perhaps relieve her of some tension. While Ruth was bathing, Ruthie kept herself busy cleaning the kitchen. She would not allow herself to think about life without Ruth. It wouldn't be a life. "Nothing was ever gained by thinking the worst," Ruth was always telling her. It was always her dear Ruth who was more positive, but once again their roles in this relationship had to flip. She would battle Ruth's enemy with love, prayer, and positive thinking.

Ruth was very tired and dropped off to sleep after the hot bath and donning the warm flannel nightgown Ruthie had brought, after warming it briefly in the dryer. Although it was early April, the temperatures dropped precipitously at night and she wanted Ruth to be as warm as possible. Ruthie got into bed with Ruth and held her until she fell asleep. It was still early as she looked at the clock, just 8 p.m. She had to talk to someone, so she went to the kitchen and quietly called the Packer home. Billy answered the phone, and when

Ruthie heard his strong, earnest voice, something about it started her crying. She choked her name out, and Billy responded, "Ruthie! Oh my god! What's the matter?" When Cindy heard Billy's side of the conversation, she jumped up from the couch and ran to Billy's side. "Ruthie, take a deep breath, and tell me what's going on?"

"Billy, our dear Ruth has breast cancer, and she is having surgery next week to remove a large malignant tumor," Ruthie managed to say in a more composed voice. "She is sleeping right now, but I just had to share this news with someone. Sorry to call you so late, but I wanted to make sure Ruth was off to sleep before I called."

Billy took a moment to clear emotion from his own voice and said, "This is whom you should be calling, my dear friend. Would you like Cindy and I to come over to your house right now?" Cindy impatiently grabbed for the phone, as Billy whispered to his wife that Ruth had breast cancer.

Ruthie heard Cindy talking to her, but she was able to take in only every other word, as her mind kept telling her this wasn't happening. "You must be an emotional wreck about this," Cindy said. "We can come right over, if you wish, dear?"

"No, Cindy; Ruth would likely wake up, and she needs to conserve her energy to fight off this damn cancer. I just thought you and Billy should know right away, being family and all. I am going to insist she call in sick tomorrow at the school district. I don't think she will fight me on this. Maybe the two of you could come by to see her tomorrow? I am going to work, because I know I will need every sick day and personal day off in the future, and it is best to save some of those days now. Hopefully, the surgery will get all the cancer and with some radiation treatments, cancer will be conquered," Ruthie said.

"That's the attitude we should all have about this right now. No need to hang our heads and start planning funeral services yet. In fact, tomorrow I will stop by just as you are leaving for work, and fix Ruth some breakfast and see if she wants to talk. She has always said that, next to you, I am her best friend, and I think she will talk to me. I'll make sure she gets proper rest. Also, I can cook dinner for the four of us when you get home from work and Billy is done with the farm chores. It would be my honor to do that, Ruthie, after all you and Ruth have done for our family, particularly our children. I am shocked, too, because Ruth did tell me about this lump, but was absolutely sure she had polycystic breasts just like her mother, and it was nothing to be worried about."

"Ironic, isn't it, Cindy? I'm usually the pessimist around here, but Ruth can't seem to play the role of the optimist right now, so I need to become one, not just for Ruth, but for my own sanity," Ruthie said. The two women ended the phone conversation as they arranged a time for Cindy's arrival in the morning.

Ruthie wasn't sleepy, so she went to the bookshelf containing their poetry and grabbed the Robert Browning volume. She flipped to the poem the two women knew by heart. "Come grow old with me! The best is yet to be." Ruthie looked in the short biography of the poet contained in the beginning of the book. It struck her that while Robert Browning lived to the age of seventy-seven, his beloved Elizabeth only lived to fifty-five. Growing old together with your beloved was every happy couple's dream, but there was no guarantee it would happen.

CHAPTER SIXTEEN

The week flew by and soon Billy was driving Cindy, Ruthie and Ruth to the hospital. They all waited just a few moments before a nurse appeared, to get Ruth ready for surgery. So Ruthie would feel more comfortable showing affection and support to Ruth, when it came time for Ruth to get in the wheelchair, both Billy and Cindy gave Ruth a quick kiss and a big hug, followed by a slightly longer embrace by Ruthie, who whispered into her ear, "I love you."

The three friends sat in the waiting room and took turns going for coffee, then sandwiches, as the time dragged on to five hours. The surgeon asked Ruth whom he should speak to about the results of the operation as she recovered from surgery, and Ruth explained who was waiting to talk to the doctor. It had been relayed to Ruth and the three waiting for her, that the operation would, probably, take about three hours at the most. After four hours, Ruthie began to pace up and down the hallways of the hospital. "Something is not right," she told Billy and Cindy. "This is taking much longer than the doctor said it would."

Finally, at the five-hour mark, the surgeon came into the waiting room and went directly to Billy. "You must be Miss Packer's cousin, Billy. Well, I am afraid the report is not the best. Your cousin came through the surgery and is in recovery now. The surgery was quite extensive. I had to remove her right breast, all the lymph nodes and part of the chest wall, as well. You may see her in about an hour. Unfortunately, she can only have one visitor at this time because she is medicated and very tired. It appears the cancer has spread to her lungs and her bones. If she does some radiation treatment in Syracuse, she probably has about six months to live. She will need to stay in the hospital about a week, and we will try to keep her as comfortable as possible with morphine and checking her dressings at least three times a day. I am so sorry about this, Mr. Packer. I can tell from my interactions with your cousin she is a brilliant, kind, and, may I say, quite an attractive lady. Too bad she is departing us in her early fifties. Any questions? The nurse will come out to get you when she is ready for a visitor."

Although they knew the news could be dire, Ruthie, Cindy, and Billy never expected this. They were momentarily speechless. Ruthie then sat down in a chair, put her head in her hands and began to cry. Cindy and Billy sat on either side of her and put their arms around her.

"Why can't it be me who has only six months? I literally have no real family, and now with Ruth leaving me, what's the point of me hanging around?" Ruthie cried.

"What do you mean you have no family, Ruthie? You are like a sister to us both, and our children adore you to death. We will always be with you right through all of this and beyond. Do you hear me?" Billy asked emphatically.

An hour later, the nurse came into the waiting room and told Billy he could see his cousin. Billy told the nurse, "I guess the surgeon did not tell you that this is also Miss Packer's cousin, Miss Stein. He talked to me primarily, and I didn't get a chance to tell him it was more appropriate for Ruthie to see my cousin in recovery. They are very close and talk about these women things better than I. I think she should go in to see Ruth. Is that okay?"

"As long as she is family, that is all that matters tonight."

With that, she escorted Ruthie toward the recovery room and Ruthie turned around, looked at Billy, and mouthed a silent "thank you." When they arrived at the room, Ruthie could see that Ruth was connected to a morphine drip as she, too, had experienced when she fell in the barn in 1964. Ruthie took a very deep breath and walked to the side of the bed facing out toward the door, so she could keep track of the comings and goings from Ruth's bedside.

Ruthie took Ruth's hand and bent down to give her a kiss on the forehead. Ruth opened her eyes and smiled. "I know all the bad news from the surgeon, so you don't need to worry about telling me anything about my condition. I was just lying here thinking about how good you were to me that first night you came into my room at the farm with the vaporizer, Vick's, hot towel, and some cough drops, because I was coughing my head off. I knew right then what a sweet soul you were. We all need someone to take care of us from time to time and you've been that person for me, always."

"You certainly paid me back a thousand times over for that slight care when you helped me recover from my fall on the concrete. I still owe you a lot of caring, only this time it is not a debt being repaid. It's my desire to be around you in every way and any way for as long as I can, because I love you so," Ruthie said as tears flowed down her cheeks once again.

"I am so sorry to put you through this, Ruthie, but from what the doctor has told me, I won't be a burden for very long. Remember, occasionally, when we were in bed, you'd call me your angel? Well, doc says I'm about to get my wings," Ruth said, with tears of her own watering her eyes.

"Please don't talk like that, Ruth. It just tears me apart. Besides, the radiation treatments might prolong your life longer than you think, and maybe God has a miracle cure in mind for you," Ruthie said.

"Ruthie, I think we only experience one or two miracles in our lifetime. I was already granted one when I met you and granted a second miracle when you did not die from that farm accident in '64. I am adamant about no radiation treatments. If those treatments are only going to add a few weeks to my life, that must be balanced against quality time being lost with you while taking all those trips to Syracuse, having all my hair fall out and continuously vomiting. The surgeon made it very clear that radiation cannot cure me of this disease."

Ruthie could not think of a reasonable answer to Ruth's careful analysis of her medical condition. No wonder Ruth won the debating team title while she was at Smith, and as her partner, Ruthie needed to put away her selfish need for having Ruth in her life for just a few more weeks, if the radiation treatment made her sicker. She looked directly into Ruth's eyes and said, "Whatever you think is best, honey." That was all she could say without bursting into tears.

Ruth went home from the hospital a week later, armed with a plethora of painkilling medication. While she had been in the hospital, Ruthie had rented a hospital bed. Although a tight fit, there was enough room to squeeze it into their bedroom overlooking their skillfully landscaped backyard, which Ruthie had completed three years ago. Ruthie also placed two bird feeders near the window and made some steps for AJ to get up onto the bed with Ruth, if she felt like having him with her.

When Ruth first walked through their back door into the kitchen, she sat at the kitchen table for a moment to catch her breath. AJ was frantically wagging his tail as he looked up at Ruth. She patted him on the head and smiled. "Thank the good Lord I made it home to spend some more time with you," Ruth said, reaching her hand out to Ruthie.

Ruthie held her hand and gave her a long kiss. "How I've missed this affection," Ruth said.

"I think, tonight, I'd like to be in our bed, Ruthie, so I can hold your hand. I know the doctor recommended the hospital bed so I can breathe easier by adjusting the head of the bed. But I am not at death's door quite yet, and being near your strength will give me strength. Lord knows I need that," Ruth said.

"You won't need to make that request twice, my dear. The closer you are to me physically, the better I will sleep. It might be best for you, anyway, to get used to the hospital bed by first taking afternoon naps in it for a few days. How about some tea before Cindy and Billy arrive with dinner?" Ruthie suggested.

"That would be great. There are many things I need to discuss with you, and it is best to do it now when others are not around. When my time comes, I do not want a funeral. I want Howard Wilson, from Wilson's funeral home, to come by the house this week, so I can pay for cremation services. I want the ashes given to you, and I hope you may honor me with holding on to them until you are buried years from now. I think they will let you put my ashes in your casket, so it can be said our earthly bodies are together forever," Ruth said.

"Do we really have to discuss this today, Ruth?" Ruthie began to tear up.

"It will never be convenient to talk about this, Ruthie,

and I will have more peace of mind knowing all has been arranged. I know there are still people at the Methodist Church who will pressure you to have a service there. But I do not want that intellectual midget, Rev. Dooley, to have any participation in any memorial, nor do I want to have him visiting me here, whatsoever. Can you keep him at bay, Ruthie?" Ruth pleaded.

"You know I will, honey," Ruthie promised.

"Ruthie, you know I am good with the Lord. You know that, don't you? That doesn't mean I am glad to be dying. There will come a time when moving past all this physical pain will help me welcome death. We all die; mine is just coming sooner than I expected and depriving me of time with you. Our times on the Cape were so glorious; I wanted more days like that with you," Ruth said.

How about we go there for Thanksgiving, sweetheart?" Ruthie suggested. "Of course, you would have to feel strong enough for the trip, but I am sure Billy and Cindy would drive us there, and Ellen could come down from Smith with her new girlfriend, Alexis."

"That would be wonderful, and I do want to see if this Alexis is good enough for our Ellen. We have the kitchen to do a whole meal for Thanksgiving, as well as two bedrooms and a sofa pull-out sleeper. What about Billy, Jr? Do you think he would come too?" Ruth asked.

"Well, he is married, and I think Cindy said Billy's wife wanted him to go to her family Thanksgiving, but they never bothered to tell Billy, Jr. that he could bring his parents and sister. Imagine that!" Ruthie said. "Will be interesting to see how that marriage turns out in the years ahead. As I often heard my father say when my late brother Walter was running about the county dating every available girl he could, 'A son's a son until he takes a wife, but a daughter is a daughter for the rest of her life.' Then Dad would smile at me and say, 'I am so glad you are my daughter, Ruthie,' with a pat on the head."

"I'll be watching the development of that marriage from heaven," Ruth smiled.

Ruthie got busy arranging everything for the Cape Cod Thanksgiving trip. She even called their Cape Cod friends, Ruby and Eileen, to see if they would like to spend Thanksgiving with them on the Cape. It was the first time Ruthie had talked to them about Ruth's cancer, and Ruby urged Ruthie to get Ruth to Sloan Kettering Hospital in New York, where she said miraculous things were being done in the field of cancer remission. When Ruby realized Ruth was months into her diagnosis, Ruby agreed it was probably too late for any treatment that would put metastatic breast cancer into remission, but they promised to journey to the Cape for Thanksgiving and offered rooms at their home for Ruth and Ruthie's relatives, if need be. They also insisted upon paying for a caterer they knew on the Cape, who would do an exceptional job of putting on the turkey feast with all the trimmings. It would be their gift to their friends they had grown to admire and love. Ruthie accepted their offer, knowing it would give her more time to sit by Ruth and tend to her every need, as her strength seemed to be waning quickly.

Ellen promised to come down from Smith with Alexis, who said she was excited about meeting Ellen's lesbian aunts whom Ellen never stopped talking about. Every Sunday since Ellen found out about Ruth's cancer, she had called Four Corners to tell her she was constantly thinking about her and wished she could stop in and have a cup of coffee or tea with her. Each time Ellen got off the phone, she had tears in her eyes. That was how she got to meet Alexis. As Ellen hung up the dormitory phone one Sunday evening, Alexis was passing by and asked Ellen if she was okay.

"No, I'm really not okay," she croaked out while blowing her nose.

"Would you like to talk to someone? I'm available, and people tell me I am a pretty good at listening, but I don't want to intrude," Alexis said, as she put a comforting hand on Ellen's shoulder. Suddenly, Ellen had a strange feeling of electricity coursing through her body. She looked right into Alexis's eyes and they reminded her of her Aunt Ruth's kind eyes.

"Don't want to take you away from studying for your

midterms," Ellen said. "If that's not the case, a cup of coffee and conversation in the canteen might be nice."

"I could study for my constitutional law midterm, but then, compared to talking with you, there is no question what I want to do. Let's get that coffee," Alexis said, as she walked beside Ellen to the canteen. Finding a private corner, she asked Ellen what she would like in her coffee and went to retrieve the java that would keep them talking late into the night.

Ellen knew about Alexis from others at Smith. Alexis was purported to be from a very wealthy Boston family. Word was that she didn't date any boys from the neighboring colleges because "she thought she was too good for them." Ellen had been in a poetry course with Alexis and had observed she was always in class, prepared and extraordinarily bright. Probably, boys were more intimidated by her intelligence and incredible beauty than Alexis pretending she was better than they were.

"So, Ellen, what's happening to make you cry?" Alexis said, as she set their coffee mugs on the table.

"It's hard to know where to begin, really. My Aunt Ruth Packer went to Smith, and in that regard, I guess I am what you would call a 'legacy.' It was some time ago she graduated from here, but she did so well that she is very much remembered by the college. She graduated summa cum laude in English literature and became a public school teacher when she could really have been an editor for one of the publishing houses in New York City. She did that because she wanted to take care of her parents in their last years. She was an only child, and they had sacrificed everything to have her at Smith, although her tuition was fully paid by Smith after her first year here.

"I'm not sure how you feel about gay people, Alexis, but my Aunt Ruth is a lesbian. You'd never know it by first appearance. She is very much the lady with earrings, beautiful clothes, and wonderful perfumes. She just happened to end up in my hometown—that is a very long story I will tell you another time, if you want. Anyway, in our town, there was another Ruth who was known by everyone as Ruthie. Ruthie was in serious need of help with her mother, who was slowly dying of congestive heart failure. Now, get this, Aunt Ruthie ran a dairy farm at that time all by herself. Yes, she was a lesbian, too, but neither of them really knew their inclination until they met. Aunt Ruth took care of Ruthie's mother for the last months of her mother's life. She also cooked and did the laundry, all the things we expect a housewife to do. Aunt Ruth had lost a teaching job to a veteran returning from the Korean War, so she needed a place to stay. Over the course of a few months, Aunt Ruth and Aunt Ruthie fell madly in love with one another and have been together for twenty-three years.

"It has always been amazing to see them together. They seem so peaceful together and so happy. Now, Aunt Ruth is dying of breast cancer and so I call her every Sunday to chat. She got me into this wonderful college, although she'd tell you, 'Oh, no, dear, I just told Smith about Four Corners' latest valedictorian.'"

Alexis took Ellen's hand and said, "How terrible is that story! What pain you must be going through. How old is your Aunt Ruth?"

"She's just turning fifty-one on November 20. My Aunt Ruthie is fifty-five," Ellen replied, as she wiped her eyes. "None of this probably makes much sense to you. Aunt Ruth is my father's first cousin, so she is my second cousin. I call her aunt because she feels like that to me, being a generation older. And since her partner is Ruthie, I call her Aunt Ruthie. My father was responsible for the two of them meeting, although he had no idea they were lesbians. In fact, my father wanted to marry Aunt Ruthie for the longest time. To this day they are best friends," Ellen explained.

"What an incredible story," Alexis said. "I could never be critical of lesbians, since I am one myself, although that hasn't yet been discussed with my parents or anyone at this school. I can see by the love you have for your aunts that you will be my confidante in that regard?" Alexis inquired.

"Of course I will," Ellen said. "I'm in the same boat as you, Alexis. The only people who know I am gay are my two aunts and my high school girlfriend, who has nothing to do with me anymore. The strain of her parents knowing about our high school relationship was just too much for her, and when we went off to college, she never returned my letters.

I think that's for the best. I've put my energy into my academics and playing field hockey," Ellen said.

Alexis studied Ellen's beautiful blue eyes and said, "Well, no wonder you are not only very pretty, but also, so physically fit. I've heard about you and your incredible math and science grades. I think someone told me you kept to yourself, mostly because you wanted to get into Cornell vet school and didn't have time for socialization. I don't suppose you'd like to go out to dinner and a movie with me sometime this week, would you?"

Ellen realized her mouth was very dry and took a sip of her coffee before saying, "I'd like that very much, Alexis. It has been lonely for me here, and I'd love to have a good friend like you who is caring enough to rescue me from my tears." With that, Ellen squeezed Alexis' hand and wrote her dormitory number on a piece of paper for Alexis. "Drop by anytime. I'm a resident advisor and have my own room. Thanks for listening tonight, Alexis."

The meeting between Alexis and Ellen occurred in the middle of September, and by mid-October they made a point to be together every day. The privacy of Ellen's room gave them a chance to explore how it felt to hold one another and kiss, but their sexual relationship had not developed much beyond what Ellen had experienced with Brenda in high school. Ellen wanted to become deeply involved with Alexis, but she assumed Alexis would move the relationship along if that was what Alexis really wanted.

The third weekend in October, Alexis indicated that her family had a cabin in the Berkshires, and she would like Ellen to accompany her there where they would be alone in the fall foliage and autumn breezes. Ellen didn't hesitate to agree to this getaway, and when she walked into the small mansion Alexis had called a cabin, she was overwhelmed at the art on the walls, the very modern kitchen, and a huge stone fireplace that was the centerpiece of the family room.

"If this is what you would call a cabin, I can't imagine what your home in Boston looks like!" Ellen said.

"Yes, I am lucky to have this so near Smith and to have you here with me," Alexis said, as she placed their backpacks on the marble floor entrance and headed to the kitchen. "Let me see if anyone has thought to leave some red wine," she said. "You would have a glass or two with me, wouldn't you?"

Ellen nodded, while still moving her eyes about the beautiful retreat. She had noticed lots of wood by the fireplace, so she assumed she'd get the pleasure of a crackling fire, which was something that always made her feel romantic. Alexis came back with two glasses of wine and directed Ellen over to the sofa facing the fireplace.

"Let me be very honest with you, Ellen. I think I am falling in love with you, and that really is not something I have ever done before, believe it or not. I also sense I have had a little more experience than you in the lovemaking department, because I had one sexual encounter with an older lesbian one summer in Provincetown. But, while it was great, and I got to experience an orgasm for the first time, it wasn't anything special. I think it would be if we made love, but I don't want to make you do anything you do not want to do. I don't believe in fooling around with lots of women. I want to find that one special woman who fills my heart with love, joy, intelligence, and peace. I think that may be you, Ellen. If you don't feel the same way about me, I understand," Alexis said, before taking a sip of her cabernet sauvignon.

Ellen couldn't quite believe what she was hearing, because it was too good to be true. How could this extremely attractive woman with black hair to her shoulders, and almost lavender colored eyes, be telling her she might love her. "Alexis, I think I fell in love with you that first time we kissed in my dorm room. On our subsequent make-out sessions, I wanted more touching but felt awkward. Brenda and I never went that far in high school," Ellen admitted sheepishly.

Alexis said with a smile, " I would love to be the first to introduce you to the world of lesbian lovemaking. But this must be a very special occasion. So, why don't we cook some pasta together, and have some of that great French bread I had delivered along with the wine before we got here this afternoon. There are also some chocolate-covered strawberries in the refrigerator for dessert. I'll make a nice fire out here for us, and we can just ease into a beautiful evening."

Ellen followed Alexis into the kitchen and helped her pull out all the ingredients, as well as pots and pans needed for their special dinner together. As Ellen sipped her wine and put the ingredients together, Alexis started a fire in the fireplace and set a table for two at the table adjacent to the roaring fire.

Their dinner was a delicious alternative to the food on campus, and Ellen thought how amazing it must be to just call up some caretaker nearby and have them go grocery shopping to fill up the fridge before they had arrived. While cooking dinner, she noticed the shopper had also secured some eggs, blueberry muffins, and orange juice for breakfast.

"Is the pasta okay?" Ellen asked?

"Just perfect—al dente," Alexis replied, as she slurped an angel hair noodle into her mouth, giggling as she did. When dinner was done, Alexis cleared the table, poured what was left of the bottle of wine into their two glasses, and told Ellen to go relax by the fire.

Once she sat next to Ellen, she put her arm around her and stared at the fire as the logs rolled down upon themselves, sending sparks everywhere. "You know, that fire kind of reminds me of us. I mean, when I first kissed you I felt a spark of energy surge through my whole body. I wanted to take you to bed right then, but told myself, 'Calm down, Alexis; this is a very special woman who deserves much respect and tenderness.'"

After those words, Alexis put her glass of wine and Ellen's glass of wine on the coffee table, and gently kissed Ellen. The kisses were returned, and before they knew what was happening they were in the king-sized bed off the family room, slowly helping each other undress.

Under the covers, Alexis began running her hands up and down Ellen's body and massaging Ellen's breasts. "What a beautiful body you have, Ellen. Strong, yet soft in all the right places." Alexis then moved her fingers between Ellen's legs as she kissed Ellen's breasts. Ellen felt a tingling sensation between her legs that she had never felt before, and before long she was shouting out, "Keep going, don't stop, I want you to use me all up." Alexis didn't stop until Ellen had exploded into a loud, "Yes, yes, yes, my love." Ellen lay quietly next to Alexis, feeling waves of pleasure flood over her.

"Was that okay?" Alexis asked. "Was I too aggressive, or did I hurt you?"

"If that is hurting me, then please sign up to be my lover forever, and hurt me every night for the rest of our lives," Ellen said, as she instinctively rolled over on top of Alexis and kissed her whole body. Soon, Alexis was moaning in pleasure as Ellen repeated the same motions Alexis had taught her. When Alexis had an orgasm, she lay still on her pillow and pulled Ellen onto her shoulder.

Throughout the night, they would drift off to sleep and then, somehow, simultaneously wake up, start kissing each other, and make love again, each time the experience seeming to reach new heights. Finally, as the sun started to peek through the curtains, they fell asleep exhausted, but addicted to each other's body.

That whole weekend was spent in love, long walks in the woods holding hands, sitting on the front porch watching the leaves dropping quietly from the trees, figuring out how they could bring their lives together forever when they graduated from Smith, and imagining growing old together. How glorious it would be to have a marriage of mind and body together, forever.

When the call came in early November from Ellen's parents asking if Ellen could drop down to the Cape for Thanksgiving with her aunts and parents, Ellen immediately told them she'd like to bring a friend named, Alexis, with her from Smith. Her mother said, "The more the merrier."

Alexis did not give it a second thought when she was asked to go to the Cape. "I really want to meet your family, and November on the Cape can be cold, but glorious, as you stroll on the deserted beaches," Alexis said.

CHAPTER SEVENTEEN

Thanksgiving 1975

Ruth began to decline rapidly as their trip to the Cape was a week away. She had to be on oxygen now, did not feel like eating, and was a mere shadow of herself. She had lost so much weight that Ruthie had no trouble moving her about in the hospital bed. She also helped Ruth get safely back and forth to the bathroom. One time, when Ruth was feeling too weak to get up for the bathroom, Ruthie picked her right up out of bed and carried her to the bathroom. Ruth hadn't lost her sense of humor and commented, "Well, there you go again, sweeping me right off my feet!"

Ruthie returned the quip, telling Ruth she would rather carry her to the bathroom, anytime, than wrestle some fire plug of a woman to the ground who was trying to hit on Ruth in the Lavender Lounge. With that, they both had a good laugh, and as Ruthie carried her back from the bathroom, Ruth suggested she put her down in their bed rather than the hospital bed, so she could cuddle up to her Sappho in Shining Armor.

Not a day went by without either Billy or Cindy dropping in to see their two friends. Cindy had been an amazing resource. She insisted on doing all their grocery shopping and was constantly cooking and baking for Ruth and Ruthie. Ruth kept talking about the trip to Cape Cod and how wonderful it would be to be near the ocean with everyone she loved. She was absolutely determined to get to Cape Cod, no matter how lousy she was feeling.

So, the Monday before Thanksgiving, their car was all packed with Ruth's oxygen's tanks, wheelchair, and fluffy pillows, as well as sandwiches and thermoses of water and coffee. Ruthie carried Ruth from the house and buckled her into the front seat. Cindy and Billy arrived just in time to follow behind in their car. Ellen called to say she had some classes to attend on Tuesday morning, but right after they were done, she and Alexis would get to the Cape before dark.

Fortunately, the weather cooperated, and although the skies were a dreary gray, the roads were bare, with little traffic to navigate. After making a couple half hour stops on the way to the Cape, they made it to their summer home just as the sun was setting. Their dear friends, Ruby and Eileen, had arrived at their summer home the Friday before, and had cleaned Ruth and Ruthie's home, put fresh linens on the beds and a vase of roses on the kitchen table, as well as supplying a variety of baked goods from the Cape bakery. They had the lights all turned on for the travelers, as well as a fire roaring in the fireplace.

Ruby and Eileen were introduced to Cindy and Billy as they helped Ruthie bring Ruth from the car in her wheelchair. Ruthie was so happy that they would have a doctor with them for Thanksgiving, because she worried about Ruth not surviving the trip.

Ellen arrived with Alexis, right on time, the next night. Ellen tried to keep to herself the horror of seeing her Aunt Ruth's physical demise. She hugged both aunts and her parents as she introduced them to Alexis. Alexis was impeccably dressed in gray wool slacks, a burgundy cashmere sweater, and a matching scarf about her neck. She shook everyone's hand and said, "Thank you for inviting me to your home for Thanksgiving. It will be so much better than the time I would have had to spend with my staid Boston clan."

Ruthie replied for the group, "Well, we are just happy you could drive our dear Ellen down from Smith. She's told us what a wonderful friend you have been to her, so it's great to meet you in person." Ruthie engulfed Alexis with one of her hugs, and the rest of the group did the same.

That evening, after all were settled into their rooms and Ruby and Eileen had left for their home, the five remaining women discussed the next day's events. Cindy had brought the fixings for blueberry pancakes for breakfast. Billy sat by the fireplace and read the *Boston Globe*, which Ruby and Eileen had delivered to Ruth and Ruthie. He occasionally glanced over at the table of women and smiled. This would be the first time in his life he had been at a family gathering where he was the only man. But he considered it a plus to be with all these women, four of whom he already adored, and Alexis was a very good-looking, well-mannered young lady. He would make sure he kept the fireplace going and chopped lots of wood while he took a mini vacation from the farm.

Once Ruthie got Ruth as comfortable as possible in a new bed Ruby and Eileen insisted on buying for them, Ruthie began the conversation. "Well, what do you think about Alexis, Ruth? Is she one of us?"

"Little doubt in my mind that is the case, and if you were to sneak out into the living room and glance over to the sofa bed, I'm sure you'd find them cuddling. As we were sitting having tea a few minutes ago, didn't you see those telling glances they were giving one another? They were the same glances we gave one another when we were first in love and socializing in public, only in Four Corners no one was sharp enough to notice us, thank God," Ruth laughed.

"Should we ask Ellen the nature of her relationship with Alexis?" Ruthie asked.

"I think they should tell us after they have talked with Cindy and Billy. Ellen's really never come out to her parents, although I do think they know she is a lesbian just like her second cousin," Ruth said. "I'll tell you one thing; I want to have a private conversation with this Alexis and try to determine if she is all she seems—smart, caring and very much smitten with our Ellen. I want to know that this is not some experimentation, or dalliance, which she is hiding from her family. Ellen went through one bad breakup, and I don't want her to have to go through another," Ruth stated emphatically. Ruth was running out of breath from talking, so Ruthie made sure her oxygen tank was adjusted correctly and took Ruth's hand as they lay, side by side, drifting off to sleep.

All awoke to the sound of wood being chopped in the side yard and the smell of blueberry pancakes Cindy was making. There was also the aroma of a special coffee brewing, which Ruby and Eileen had brought from New York. They had indicated to everyone that they were addicted to the brand, Chock Full o' Nuts, and hoped the Four Corners crew would find it equally tasty.

Ellen yawned as she crawled slowly out of the sofa bed and left Alexis sleeping soundly. She went into the kitchen and gave her mother a big hug. "If that coffee tastes as good as it smells, then the TV ads are correct that it is 'that heavenly coffee,'" Ellen said.

"Why don't you and I have a cup together before I make any more pancakes? Your dad is chopping enough wood for the whole Cape. I imagine Ruth and Ruthie will be up in a few minutes. The coffee is done." Cindy poured a mug full for each, and they sat down at the small breakfast table.

Cindy just took one gulp of her coffee and then looked right into Ellen's eyes, asking, "Okay, so what's up with you and Alexis?"

Ellen was a little bit surprised to be confronted by her mother this way, but now was as good a time as ever to talk to her about the gay issue. "Well, Mom, we've never really talked about it, but I believe you must know I am a lesbian just like aunts Ruth and Ruthie. I am not ashamed of that, because they have taught me I can live an honorable and productive life as a lesbian, especially if I find the right partner," Ellen offered in a very cautious tone.

"Yes, my dear, I have suspected you were a lesbian since high school. I suppose you have shared that fact, and much more, with your beloved aunts, and I am glad you have. I am not unhappy about you being a lesbian; I just worry about your future and what hatred you might encounter. That Anita Bryant in Florida is stirring up quite a storm about the homosexual community, and most people start quoting the Bible when they find out you are gay or lesbian. I just want you to have a great life. You are the light of my life, Ellen. You are brilliant, kind, and very pretty. Oh sure, it would be nice to be a grandmother to your children, but from the looks of things, your brother is going to provide me with lots of grandchildren to fuss over. I want to know that you will not let Alexis break your heart," Cindy said, with a look of concern.

"Well, Mom, I am sure I am in love with her, and I am

not exactly a baby anymore. I am twenty-one, and so is she. We know what we are doing and the consequences of trying to form a life together. Don't you like her, Mom?" Ellen turned her head and glanced at the sleeping Alexis. "Isn't she gorgeous?"

"I will give you that for sure; she is beautiful, and from our brief encounter last night, it is evident she is brilliant, from a wealthy family, and down-to-earth. She wants to be an attorney, from what I understand, and her father went to Harvard Law." Cindy said. "How's that going to work out with you going off to Cornell Veterinary School? You're still planning to do that, aren't you?"

"We don't have all the pieces worked out yet, but we do want to be together forever. Yes, of course, I will go to Cornell if I get in. I'm still waiting to hear about that. Alexis says she's going to apply to Cornell Law, even if her dad is upset with her not going to Harvard. There is no doubt she could get in at Harvard, but she wants to set her own course in life. Cornell is still Ivy League, and she thinks she'll probably work for the ACLU when she graduates. The ACLU would be delighted to have a Cornell graduate," Ellen explained.

"Do her parents know she is gay? Wouldn't they be upset if they find that out, and learn that, rather than follow her father in Harvard Law, and then into his prestigious Boston law firm, she heads off to the ACLU? I am just worried her family's pressure to conform will be too much, and you will have your heart broken again, just like you did in high school," Cindy said, as she once again looked directly into Ellen's eyes.

"You knew about Brenda? Did Aunt Ruth or Aunt Ruthie tell you all about that?" Ellen asked?

"Are you kidding? Those aunts of yours were tight-mouthed about that situation. But, I am your mother, and I am not naïve. I watched your spirits nose dive after you two stopped hanging around one another. I was actually happy you spent a lot of time with Ruth and Ruthie, because I knew they would understand, keep you studying, and help you go on with your life," Cindy smiled, as she poured her daughter another cup of coffee.

Alexis was up and dressed as she approached the kitchen, aware of the intense conversation occurring between Ellen and her mom. "She knows, Alexis, that we are a couple," Ellen said with a smile.

Alexis walked over to Ellen and put her hand on Ellen's shoulder while looking at Cindy. "I love your daughter, Mrs. Packer. I love her more than I thought it was possible to love anyone. She is so bright, yet so humble about her brilliance. She is kind and thoughtful. Her integrity is beyond reproach. I want us to be together forever, and I promise you I will do everything I can to make her life happy and secure," she said.

"I trust you will be true to your word, and Lord help you if you are not, because there are two lesbians in that bedroom who will make your life miserable, without me even asking them to do so, if you break my Ellen's heart," Cindy warned.

"I know that, Mrs. Packer. Ruth said she wanted to talk to me privately sometime today, and I think that would be an interrogation, rather than a friendly conversation. That's fine with me. I would be disappointed for Ellen if she didn't have these women in her life who love her so much and want the best for her. It is okay to quiz me and see if I meet with their approval," Alexis said.

Soon, everyone was up for the blueberry pancake special. The conversation was lively as they discussed the wonder of the Cape, how fortunate they all were to have one another in their lives, and what special plans Alexis and Ellen had after their graduation from Smith. Ruth was clearly struggling to talk, and so Ruthie helped her eat a few more bites of the pancakes and then pulled her wheelchair back from the table, as Ruthie did the same with her chair. She then put her arm around Ruth and made sure Ruth was wrapped up in her blanket. After a few minutes, Ruth said she thought she might like to lie back down in her bed for a while, but wanted to talk to Alexis. Billy took his cousin to her bed and gently lifted her from the wheelchair to the bed as Ruthie watched, a tear running down her cheek. She thought about how much she loved Billy for all that he had done for her, and especially for bringing Ruth into her life.

Once Ruth was propped up on her pillows, Alexis

entered the room. Ruth invited Alexis to sit in the chair right next to her bed and to take her hand.

"My dear, I know you and Ellen are in love. Quite truthfully, I've never seen Ellen so happy. I know you are brilliant, wealthy, sophisticated, and well-connected. You obviously know how extraordinarily smart my Ellen is, but she is not sophisticated, well-connected, or wealthy. You come from different worlds, and I worry that in the long haul of life, this will be an impediment to lifelong commitment. We all need to find our own way in life, and sometimes life has a way of humbling us to the point we want to give up. If you intend to spend your life with Ellen, do not promise that to her unless you really mean you will work past the obstacles the two of you encounter, no matter what.

"Lord knows Ruthie and I have had an extraordinary relationship. I love that woman more now than when we first made love to one another. We became soulmates, and we never fell in love with anyone else, because when we were in each other's arms, we knew that was what had been predestined for us. I think you do love my Ellen very much, by the way I watched the two of you last night, and again at the breakfast table. I am not long for this world, as you know, but I want to look down upon you two and see that same passion Ruthie and I have had," Ruth said, as she started to cough and ran out of breath.

"Miss Packer, I am honored you would take this time

to talk with me. I am madly in love with Ellen and, while our lovemaking is extraordinary, so are our quiet moments together. We will always be the best of friends; I can tell just by our short time dating. I promise you, with my whole heart, that I will not take Ellen's kindness and gentle disposition for granted. And, if I do, send a lightning bolt my way from beyond, to shock me back into my senses?" Alexis said. With that, Ruth smiled and brought Alexis' hand to her lips for a kiss. She then asked Alexis to get Ellen.

Ellen came into Ruth's bedroom with tears streaming down her cheeks. While Alexis was with Ruth, Ellen's parents and Ruthie contemplated this might be Ruth's last day, since she was having such a difficult time breathing. Ellen sat on the edge of the bed and took Ruth's hand.

"Don't cry, Ellen. It's okay. Passing on to the next existence will be relief from the terrible pain I am feeling now, but I don't want any pain medication just yet. There is something very important I want you to promise me. Okay, dear?" Ruth whispered, with the little bit of breath she had left. "Please take care of your Aunt Ruthie like you would your own mother, Ellen. She's going to take my leaving her very hard and will isolate herself away from the world, if your family lets her do it." Barely able to talk, Ruth pushed out the words with great effort. "Ruthie is the finest woman on the face of the earth. She has given me more love than anyone could have ever given me. We truly adored one another and made it through some tough times, because that adoration for each other was a constant. I am so proud of you, Ellen, and so is Ruthie. So please take care of her for me. Will you promise me that?" Ruth asked.

"Oh, Aunt Ruth. Even if you hadn't asked me to do that, I would have done it anyway. You know I love Aunt Ruthie. All those long walks she used to take me on when I was a child, explaining so much about nature to me, it bonded me to her forever. Even on our farm, I tried to fashion myself after Aunt Ruthie, physically working hard and loving those farm animals. I will always look after her, and when she is too feeble to live on her own, she will live with me, I promise," Ellen replied, as she choked back more tears.

Ruth faintly called "Ruthie?" Ellen raced into the living room and retrieved Ruthie.

As Ruthie approached Ruth's side of the bed, Ruth patted Ruthie's side of the bed instead. Ruthie moved around the bed and lay next to Ruth. Ruth whispered, "Put my head on your shoulder." Ruthie did as Ruth requested and brought Ruth's thin body tight against her own. "Not much of a Thanksgiving for you, sweetheart," Ruth weakly said.

Ruthie silently asked God for strength. "Ruth, Thanksgiving is more than turkey and pumpkin pie. It is supposed to be about feeling grateful for all our blessings. Until I see you again, honey, every Thanksgiving will remind me that God sent me an angel to love and now I am just turning you over to your rightful owner. How often does one get a chance to live with an angel for twenty-three years?" Ruthie said, as she gently caressed Ruth's hair.

Ruth smiled, and then she was gone.

CPSIA information can be obtained
at www.ICGtesting.com
Printed in the USA
FSHW010509131218
54436FS